PORTRAIT

OF A

SHADOW

Praise for

A GUIDE TO THE DARK

"Metoui masterfully handles perspective . . . themes of grief, fraught and romantic queer connections to a friend, and familial expectations are thoughtfully explored."

—*The Bulletin of the Center for Children's Books*

"A ghostly mystery and an impactful exploration of grief and loss."

—*Publishers Weekly*

"Introspective, character-driven, and—most importantly—haunting."

—*Kirkus Reviews*

"Terrifically haunting. *A Guide to the Dark* delves into the complexities of grief and the frightening metamorphosis of ghosts that aren't put to rest. Meriam Metoui has created something spectacular."

—**Chloe Gong**, #1 *New York Times*–bestselling author of *These Violent Delights*

"Meriam Metoui's exquisite debut is a bone-chilling story about grief, guilt, and what happens when our deepest secrets refuse to stay hidden in the dark. *A Guide to the Dark* will crawl under your skin and stay there long after you've closed its pages."

—**Aiden Thomas**, #1 *New York Times*–bestselling author of *Cemetery Boys* and *The Sunbearer Trials*

PORTRAIT
OF A
SHADOW

MERIAM METOUI

Henry Holt and Company
New York

Henry Holt and Company, *Publishers since 1866*
Henry Holt® is a registered trademark of Macmillan Publishing Group, LLC
120 Broadway, New York, NY 10271 • fiercereads.com

Our books may be purchased in bulk for promotional, educational, or business use. Please contact your local bookseller or the Macmillan Corporate and Premium Sales Department at (800) 221-7945 ext. 5442 or by email at MacmillanSpecialMarkets@macmillan.com.

Library of Congress Control Number: 2023948950

First edition, 2024
Book design by L.Whitt
Printed in the United States of America

ISBN 978-1-250-86327-0
10 9 8 7 6 5 4 3 2 1

TO NIDHI PUGALIA,
WHO FOUND ME WANDERING
THE WILDWOOD AND
HANDED ME A MAP

The only way to get rid of a temptation is to yield to it.

—**Oscar Wilde**, *The Picture of Dorian Gray*

The Beginning

1891

There is a stillness in the air she cannot place, as if time has frozen and forgotten her. The sparrows that sing this early in the morning are muffled, like she is listening to them through water. When the sun lights the dark hardwood floor, the dust motes dance in place, basking in the rays for a little while longer than they have any right to. Delphine can see this, can hear the birdsong in ways she never could before. And suddenly, she knows she shouldn't be privy to this surreal, unexplainable moment, that maybe it isn't hers to take. When she tries to explain it to a friend later that night, she will fail to describe the stillness that surrounded her. Will not come close to depicting the disconcerting sensation of being in her own skin.

As quickly as it came, the moment passes. She returns to the canvas and, brush in hand, regards her finally dry and freshly framed self-portrait. Finished, at last. The woman that glares back is mesmerizing in her intensity, her gaze piercing and relentless. Delphine knows that it is her best work to date. And yet, she finds that once complete, it looks more like her than herself. She cannot bear to look at it or part with it, and so the only way to escape it is to efface it from existence.

Before she can hesitate, she dips the thick-bristle brush into the can of white paint at her feet and, in wide, sweeping strokes, disappears. She steps back to take in her work. The gold frame is newly brushed and polished, and in the morning light, it shines. Peculiar in its emptiness, the painting seems to take up more room than it should. More room than is possible. For a moment, she is convinced that there is nothing left in this space, that it is entirely made up of a white painting framed in gold. She shakes her head and sets her brush down. She is having a strange morning. All she needs is some fresh air, she is certain. And so, she leaves the confines of her studio and the painting that stands in the middle of it—its clean, careful strokes, barely intelligible as they dry, here, for the first time.

All but a corner that begins to unfurl, the dark paint beneath gleaming in the sun.

Chapter 1

Inez is missing, and missing things can always be found. Mae knows this as fact, even if her parents and the police have all but given up.

"I can go."

The words tumble out of her mouth faster than she can think them.

Her mom stares at her for a second, trying to decide if she is serious.

"Let me call you back," she says to the phone at her ear. She turns to Mae. "You don't have to do that, habibti. You shouldn't have to," she says, switching to Arabic. She sets the phone down and goes back to wiping the kitchen counter. The black granite shines beneath her rag.

"I know. But it doesn't feel right to let a stranger do it. They're her things. She wouldn't want that." She tries not to sound too eager, tries not to give herself away, but Mae has spent months under the too-close supervision of her overprotective parents, months hoping for an opportunity to go to the apartment, and finally, here is one for her to grab. She wouldn't pass it up. Inez's whole life is in that studio, and Mae is not about to let a donation company go through it like it's trash, not when there's even the smallest chance that the police missed something.

Her mother stops wiping for a second and stares at her. "Maybe I can take off work next week and we can go together?"

Mae can see her mentally going through her week, trying to figure out what shift to request off at the hospital, what nurses to ask to cover, but Mae isn't oblivious. She knows why her sensible, often frugal, parents would rather hire someone to go through Inez's apartment than do it themselves. As complicated as their relationship with their eldest daughter had been, her disappearance changed things. The anger they'd let harden in the five years since Inez abruptly left home melted away the second they got that phone call in December.

Well, not so much melted as it was redirected. It's clear her parents blame each other for Inez's disappearance. For months, Mae has been tiptoeing around them, as if waiting for a bomb to go off. When she listens closely, she can hear the ticks in the heavy silences between her parents—every misplaced word or too-quick glance, a moment closer to ruin. They are both always on edge, looking for an opportunity to go on the attack. Mae can't help but wonder how long they can be on that edge before they fall off.

If only their mother hadn't pushed Inez away all those years ago.

If only their father listened instead of made demands.

If only. If only.

When they aren't fighting with each other, they're fighting

with Mae. Paranoia is a guest in their home, and they are both convinced Inez's fate is Mae's to share, that if she isn't home by a certain time, if she doesn't pick up by the second ring, if they fail to save her from herself, they will lose her too. It's been easier to go into herself, to stop asking to go out, to stop saying yes to plans. People have stopped calling to make them, and she's been fine with that if it means keeping the peace. But this is different. This is important. Inez. Her things. She couldn't live with herself if she didn't at least try. No one knows Inez better than Mae, so if some stray clue or lead has been missed, Mae will be the one to find it. As the search for Inez dwindled to nothing, Mae's need to go herself only grew. For months, she bided her time, looking for any excuse to slip out for a day without raising suspicion, but her parents questioned every lie, resisted every request. Today, the perfect opportunity has fallen into her lap. There is no choice but to take it.

"Don't. I can go today. It's summer vacation. I'm not even doing anything."

"Go where?" her dad says as he walks into the kitchen.

"Brooklyn. To pack up Inez's apartment." Her mother fills him in.

"That's what we hired the donation company for."

"I know that's what we scheduled a pickup with the donation company for," she says through gritted teeth.

"Seriously, I want to do this. It's fine. I'll pack up some of her stuff to bring back, and the donation company can deal with the rest. We can't let them throw everything away. Please." She jumps in quickly. There is a small window before things escalate, before this opportunity disappears as quickly as it came. She needs to go, and if she's being honest, she needs to go alone. She doesn't think she can handle an entire day spent between their bickering. Not to mention all the pitying looks from two people who are convinced she is delusional for thinking Inez will be back for her things. Maybe she's lost in the Amazon Rainforest, living off rainwater and mangoes, Mae thinks. Or lost her memory in some freak accident and is going by Sophia Smith, a girl Mae wouldn't recognize who loves crossword puzzles and small towns. Would it be so hard to imagine it as true?

Their faces soften as they look at each other, deciding in silence. Her mom's set jaw, her dad's furrowed brow, gone, as they communicate in whatever dead language only they speak. Mae doesn't let this moment of peace tug at her heart. It is too fleeting, too small. She knows the dreaded D-word has loomed over all of them for months. But neither will admit how miserable they are, and so the misery continues. Mae is *this* close to filing their divorce papers herself, but she feels guilty for even thinking it. She just wants for this to not feel so hard. For any of them.

Finally, her mom nods.

"Be back before dark. I mean it, Mae. Just there and back, and you call us when you get there and when you leave," she says.

Mae expects to feel relief, but instead, a sudden wave of panic threatens to take her under. She can feel it in the way her heart thuds too fast, how her hands have gone clammy. It is one thing to want this, another to have it. Their *yes* means she'll have to go to Inez's apartment, to see her signs of life and know that if she doesn't sift through them in just the right way, Inez will be lost forever. She doesn't know if she should thank them or say *never mind* and lock herself in her room for the rest of the summer. Instead, she nods and leaves to grab her things. Each step feels heavier than the last. Like if she doesn't move fast enough, the quicksand will swallow her whole. She just needs to make it down the hall and to the left. She just needs to grab her backpack and head out. To New York.

To Inez's apartment.

The thought alone feels weighty, but if she dwells on it too long, she'll sink. And so, she puts one step in front of the other and reminds herself of the only truth she is willing to believe: Inez is alive and well. She will be back, and she will have an explanation for the past seven months.

"Mae, wait," her dad says, following her into her room. "Here. Take my car."

She looks at the keys in his outstretched hand with surprise. She doesn't know why he trusts her with his car. She barely trusts herself with hers.

"Are you sure?"

"It's a three-hour drive and your car isn't built for that."

She takes the keys, already regretting it. Driving to New York is going to be nerve-racking enough, so why not add potentially crashing her dad's barely year-old car to the list.

"Thanks." She tucks them into her backpack and continues searching her room for the rest of her things. Wallet, phone, headphones, sketchbook, pencils. Things she never leaves home without.

A few seconds later, he is still there. She looks at him, waiting. Her dad never talks about Inez leaving home. It isn't that he avoids the topic. He's just never the one to bring it up. Which is why Mae is surprised when he says her name.

"Inez loved you."

She flinches at his use of past tense. Why is it so easy for everyone to give up on Inez?

"I wouldn't have to go if you guys kept paying for the apartment," she says, changing the subject.

"You know we can't, Mae. Your mom's been working double shifts for months trying to pay for it." He usually avoids talking about money with Mae, but there is no avoiding this. "We took out a loan to cover the rest. We just can't keep doing this." He pauses for a moment before quietly continuing. "I'm not giving up on her. But I also can't keep staring at the front door all day, expecting her to walk through it. It just—it hurts too much."

Mae sighs. How is it that the same hope that gets her through the day is the one he can't take any more of? Yet, when he says things like that, she can't help the way her anger comes loose. All that's left is a hollow ache, and the reminder that the only person she's truly mad at is herself. Maybe if she didn't spend so much time keeping the peace, she wouldn't be getting ready to pack up her sister's apartment. She should have forced the three of them into a room together, parent trapped them all until they bridged this years-long chasm. Maybe it would have changed things.

"There are empty boxes in the garage you can take with you. Call us if you need anything, okay?"

She nods, grabs her backpack, and hugs him goodbye. Her mom is on the phone when she goes downstairs, and so she waves and heads out the back door to the garage.

The black SUV beeps and flashes as she unlocks it. Behind two sleds and a nearly forgotten bike are the boxes, dusty but sufficient. She stuffs them in the trunk and begins her trek to Brooklyn. It only takes a few minutes to make it out of Benton, Pennsylvania, unsurprising considering the town has a population of 754. Looking at the sign, she does not understand how her parents can blame Inez for leaving, and to New York City of all places. Even at thirteen, Mae knew that was a feat. But it doesn't matter. They cannot see Inez for all she is. Inez, who wants so much from the world and knows all she must do is take it. Up until last December, Inez had been in New York working on her master's degree in art history at NYU. But according to her Arab parents, there are some things an unmarried girl doesn't do. Moving away from home is one of them, apparently punishable by excommunication. Mae has given up trying to understand it. She avoids thinking about how it applies to her own question mark of a future, about where *she* may end up, if they will approve, and what it would mean if they didn't.

Back then, Mae put it all aside and visited Inez in secret the second she started driving, planning frequent day trips and foolishly hoping their parents would eventually figure their shit out. They never did. But that's okay, Mae tells herself now. Because this time around she is going to force them to resolve this before another five years go by. And they will resolve it. Mae will make sure of it. Because Inez is coming back.

The mountains race past her, and for a moment, she is on her way to see Inez. These are, after all, the same trees, same signs, that she drove past each time. Why does this drive have to feel any different? Why couldn't she be about to enter New York, ready to spend another day in Washington Square Park with her sister before they make their way to their favorite ramen spot on Fourth Street? They would finish their bowls and take the Q train home, with plans to cuddle up on the couch with ice cream and a movie on Inez's laptop as rain drummed against the windows. Mae would pack her things as the credits rolled, and they'd hug goodbye before Mae made the drive back home, her parents none the wiser.

But instead, here she is, three hours later and alone, anxiety a pit in her stomach as the city buzzes around the car. It is all too fast, too sudden, like if she isn't careful, the city would devour her whole and she'd disappear between its cracks. Her grip on the steering wheel tightens every minute she has to drive through New York. She never enjoys driving, but this? This is something else. New York weaves around her faster and faster. This is the third time she's driven around the block looking for a parking spot. Finally, like the gods have taken pity on her, a yellow Ford Focus slips into traffic and a spot opens.

Mae has to take a deep breath before she attempts to parallel park for the first time in two years, a skill she abandoned as soon as she passed her driver's test. In her rearview mirror, a bus approaches. Quickly, she twists the steering wheel and reverses into the spot, but halfway in, she knows it's all wrong. She inches out of it to try again, and by now the bus is honking, one long, blaring horn. She considers abandoning it, driving up a block or two to look for another, but instead, she grips the steering wheel a little tighter and sits up. Sweat pours down her back as she tries again, her turn wider this time, her reverse slower. She twists the wheel back and aligns her car with the sidewalk. It feels like a miracle when the bus continues past her. One quick glare from the driver and it's gone.

She turns off the car, her heart pounding, and rests her head on the steering wheel.

A few feet away from where she's collapsed in her seat is the last place Inez was. As much as she wants to think of Inez gallivanting across the world with no reception to speak of, she is scared that being in her apartment, seeing her unmade bed and and folded laundry, yet to be put away, proof of her interrupted life, will only make Mae think the worst. Like how she could have been taken or trapped in some murderer's basement. Or worse. No. She cannot think about that right now. Right now, she needs to air out her armpits, take a deep breath, and get inside Inez's apartment. One overwhelming task at a time. She picks up her phone from the charger and pulls up their messages.

Visiting you is a lot more fun than visiting your empty apartment. Come back already, she texts.

None of the messages from the past seven months are listed as seen, but it hasn't stopped Mae from sending them. She scrolls up through their thread. It takes a while to find Inez's last text.

Call me.

By the time Mae did, it was too late.

She snaps herself out of it and opens the car door as a taxi swerves to avoid her. The driver yells out profanities, but Mae doesn't hear them. The moment she steps away from the AC, the summer humidity smacks her, made worse than usual by a particularly persistent heat wave hitting the East Coast. She grabs her backpack, slams the door, and carefully inspects the car, relieved to find she hasn't scratched it. The trip back will be another ordeal, but for now, she will take this as a win.

She quickly grabs the flat boxes from the trunk before jumping onto the sidewalk, but the pedestrians are no better than the cars as Mae finds herself jostled back and forth. An older woman shoulder-bumps her as she speed-walks toward the crosswalk, making Mae—and her boxes—teeter wildly to the side. A man glares as he maneuvers around her, grumbling to himself. She steadies herself with a focused breath, fresh sweat pouring down her forehead. Mae never liked the city much. Brooklyn, Manhattan, it was all the same to her. She felt so small in all of it. *Why would anyone want to call this place home?* she had asked Inez before. Inez had shrugged and smiled. *I can't explain it. It's this breathing thing. Being here reminds me I am too.*

Mae and her sister are different in almost every way she can name. Mae is a gangly 5'8" with chin-length wavy brown hair and bangs she has no idea what to do with. Inez is a few inches shorter—something Mae loves to make fun of her for. Her long curly hair that she got from their mom is as wild as she is. Inez is the exciting one, always off on a new adventure. She always knows what she wants and how to get it. Mae, on the other hand, at a freshly minted eighteen, still cannot answer the dreaded *what do you want to be when you grow up* question. She's not sure there is a future for her where she can.

Now that high school is over, Mae is an arrow with no target. Her parents never fail to steer her in any direction they find appropriate. *What about an engineer? An architect? You're creative. A lawyer? A doctor? You love helping people!* She mostly tunes them out until they exhaust themselves. But Inez isn't like that. Inez never tries to suggest things like everyone else. So intent on helping, no one sees Mae is overwhelmed by the choices, not the lack of them. Inez sees that, lets her accept it. She is convinced her little sister will figure it out herself, even if Mae still isn't so sure.

The last time they talked was a few weeks before she went missing. Mae had sent Inez a rambling, panic-induced message about college applications being due and how she had no idea what she was doing or how to tell her parents she didn't want any of it. Instead of replying, Inez called her.

"You're fine. Take a deep breath. They're not going to shun you," she said. It was the unspoken worry in the air. One Mae didn't have the heart to put to words. But Inez knew. She always knew.

"I don't know if that's true."

"One daughter and they can blame the kid, but both and they have to blame their parenting. I promise, they'll get over it." Mae could see Inez's grim smile, even over the phone.

"Okay, okay, I can take a gap year and they will get over it."
She wasn't sure if she believed it just yet, but maybe if she said
it aloud, she would will it into truth.

Before Inez had a chance to reply, someone in the back-
ground said, "Dinner's ready."

"Are you with someone? Dealing with my meltdown could
have waited."

"No, no. I'm alone. That's just the TV." A second later, Mae
could swear she heard someone call for her sister.

"I do have to go though, I'll talk to you later, okay?"

They said their goodbyes, and Mae made a mental note to
ask if Inez was seeing anyone next time she talked to her. She
never got the chance.

No.

She will focus on one crisis at a time. And packing up Inez's
apartment will take up all her mental space. There is nothing
left of herself to give.

She walks down the narrow hallway, up the stairwell to the
second floor, and prepares herself for what she is about to see.
In December, her parents came alone. She had stayed home,
too afraid to see the studio, the parts of Inez left behind, the
signs of life without her there. She remembers staying in bed,
watching episode after episode of a show she couldn't remember, just so she wouldn't have to be alone with her thoughts.

It was her the cops had called first. She was listed as Inez's
emergency contact on her school paperwork, and when Inez
didn't show up to class, a friend reported her missing. Most of
the call is a blur. Mae was silent on the phone, nodding until

she finally remembered the cop couldn't see her. Finally, she stammered out a thank-you and slowly set the phone down.

"Inez. They—they can't find her."

Her parents just stared at her. Then, with the world on mute, they whirled around her, figuring out what to do next. They led her to her room, and she didn't come out for days. But she has avoided the inevitable long enough.

She takes a breath, steels herself, and is surprised to find the gray door ajar, light falling against the carpeted hallway in one long streak. She tiptoes toward it, careful not to make a sound as she slips through the open doorway. As Mae scans the room, she has the sinking feeling that she isn't alone.

Chapter 2

The boy jumps at the sound of the creaking hardwood beneath her feet. On the desk next to him, a half-full watering can falls to the floor. They both pause to look at the water slowly collecting near his shoes before he turns back to her.

"Who are you?" he asks. The boy, no older than twenty, leans against a black cane. At the top is a silver rabbit head, its ears long and pulled back. Beneath it, a snake wraps around the wood. It's difficult to see where the dark wooden cane ends and where the black metal snake begins.

"Really feel like I should be the one asking that question. What are you doing in my sister's apartment?"

"Sister? Inez doesn't ha—" He trails off as his eyes widen. "You're Inez's sister." It isn't a question this time. She nods.

"Mae." She isn't sure why she answers his not-question. For all she knows, he could be robbing the place. Maybe he broke in and was in the middle of ransacking the apartment when she showed up. "And you are?"

"Dev." The water finally reaches the soles of his white

sneakers, and he jumps to grab a towel hanging on the stove handle a few feet away.

He seems frazzled as he slowly bends down to wipe the mess he's made. His wavy dark hair falls over his eyes, but he quickly runs his fingers through it to keep it at bay. He's cute, in a brown James Dean sort of way, Mae thinks. His black short-sleeve button-up hugs his arms well, one side loosely tucked into black jeans. He's managed to have the top two buttons unbuttoned and still not look like an asshole. She is impressed.

"Okay, that answers the who. Now, *what* are you doing here, Dev?"

"I look after her plants from time to time," he says as he soaks up the water. She folds her arms as she takes in the brown leaves barely clinging on to the pothos behind him. Next to it, a parched succulent hangs on for dear life.

"So, what, you broke in to make sure my sister, who hasn't lived here since December, still has her plants watered?"

His ears turn pink as he looks at her with mild indignation. "I have a key."

Mae looks at him for a while before she decides to let it go. Inez must have trusted him, Mae thinks, at least enough to give him a copy of her key. But still. Mae isn't sure she can just yet. He could be lying. Strangers do that, even attractive ones. Especially attractive ones, she guesses. She keeps an eye on him as she shuts the front door and leans the flat boxes against the wall, but he seems busy with the mess he's made.

She takes a minute to look around the place. It's as if Inez has stepped away for a moment, like she has run downstairs to check the mail and will come back and throw the unopened letters on the kitchen counter, her keys clattering as she tosses them onto the granite. If only Mae stares at the door long enough, wills it enough. But the door stays shut, and aside from the squeak of Dev's shoes, the room is silent. It is getting harder to convince herself of what these remnants deny.

An empty cup rests on the low coffee table. Next to it is a delicate and frayed copy of *The Picture of Dorian Gray* splayed open; its brittle spine stays bent even when she picks it up. Mae flips it over to see a neat scrawl on the title page: *I lost this book on a train. When I found it again years later, it felt like fate. Meeting you felt a lot like that.* There's no signature, no name. She checks the copyright page and finds that she's holding a first edition, printed in 1891. She doesn't understand why her sister would have this, who would give it to her, or what it means, if anything. Inez had never mentioned seeing anyone for more than a date or two. Mae closes the book and gently places it back on the table. A few feet away is Inez's unmade bed, her bright yellow duvet half on the floor. The place is bare, and though she should have had roommates, she sacrificed a lot for this studio. She is good at being alone. Mae doesn't know how to be.

She looks around and only then notices that the overhead light is on, a strange, sharp brightness in the middle of the day. The blackout curtains are drawn on the two windows in the entire apartment, and when Mae goes to push them open, she realizes Inez has nailed them to the wall, not a single sliver of sunlight escaping through. Mae doesn't know what to make of it. The fabric is thick, dark. Why fix them to the wall?

"I didn't know she had anyone."

"What do you mean?" she says, turning around to find Dev staring at her. He looks sad to say it. Like Inez's loneliness is something she carries with her, like it is all she has for company. Mae thinks of the note, of someone that Inez hadn't mentioned to either of them. Maybe the note wasn't to her, then. Just a gift between two lovers until she found it in a used bookstore somewhere.

"Just that Inez always kept to herself. She never mentioned anyone. I always thought she was an only child. I could swear she'd said that once."

"Oh." She isn't sure what to say to this. Inez had her. She thought her sister had known that, but maybe she hadn't. Maybe she felt more alone here than Mae realized.

"She's never mentioned you either. How do you know her?"

"We're neighbors. I live next door."

She nods her head, smiles a polite smile. They look around the apartment for a moment, letting the silence build.

"You look like her, you know."

His brown eyes meet hers, and she is suddenly aware of the sweat-soaked armpits of her black crop top, barely hidden by oversize burgundy overalls with a stain on the strap from the last time she wore them. She grabs a box to busy her hands, and maybe to cover the sweat.

"You're the first to think so." With Inez's curls and Mae's height, her lighter skin tone and Mae's olive, nobody ever looks at them and thinks they are sisters. It's nice to be seen, she thinks.

"You have the same smile."

"Thanks." She looks away, as if that would hide the blush creeping up her cheeks.

"You haven't heard from her, have you?" she asks after a few quiet seconds. She knows the answer, but a part of her braces anyway.

He shakes his head. "I was away. I just heard she was missing. Thought I'd come back and check in on her place."

"Well, you won't need to water her plants anymore," Mae says, motioning toward the watering can he has set aside on the kitchen counter. "A, her plants are all dead. And B, I'm here to pack up her things. My parents—"

"What?" His eyes go wide for a second as he looks around the room. "They really think she's not coming back?" he asks, his eyebrows raised.

Something in her softens, and she feels a bit of the wariness she holds toward him fall away. What a relief to know he isn't assuming she is dead, that a fellow skeptic is holding out hope she'll make her way back to them. That Inez isn't lost, just momentarily misplaced.

Mae shakes her head and hopes he understands the rest.

He nods and looks around the studio. "Why don't I help you? You'd finish in half the time."

She takes in Inez's practically empty apartment, which is somehow still a mess. Mae doesn't really need the help. And yet. The thought of being in this apartment alone suddenly feels overwhelming.

She nods and hands him a box. "If you insist."

He walks toward Inez's thin bookcase and sets his cane against the shelves before bending down to sit on the floor. He folds open the box into itself and starts lining it with her books. Tattered romance novels, art history hardcovers—the shelves seem to sigh with the weight of it all. Mae wants so badly to flip through them and look for notes in the margins. A dog-eared page or tea-stained cover. She'll take anything at this point. They've never gone this long without talking. After Inez had gone off to college, Mae powered through the books she left behind. The more annotated they were, the more Mae knew she loved them. And now, here is history repeating itself. With Mae searching for scraps of Inez in what she left behind.

Dev picks up a book and smiles, turning it over in his hands before placing it in the box. What does *he* know about her that Mae doesn't? What sides of her is he familiar with that she is still a stranger to? For one fleeting moment, Mae imagines ripping the book out of his hands and demanding he tell her every secret thing about Inez she never bothered to share with Mae.

She looks away. Mae could begin packing, lining the wall with filled boxes, but that's not why she's made it all this way. Not really. There are answers to be found, and so she begins with the obvious. She walks over to Inez's dresser and begins pulling open the drawers, moving Inez's collection of concert T-shirts in search of something. Anything.

He eyes her, and she knows how this looks. It isn't packing.

"Are you looking for something? Did she steal a dress you're trying to get back?" he says as he folds a box of books closed.

She rolls her eyes and keeps rummaging through the drawers.

Nothing. "Do you ever see someone screw something up and you just watch, knowing you could do a better job, if only you had the chance?"

"Sure," he says, stretching out the word, but his eyes are narrowed and it's clear he's not sure what she's getting at.

She walks over to the now-bare bookshelf and runs her hands across the top. "I'll start packing, but first, I need to see what I can find that the cops didn't." Finds only dust.

"Why? Did it seem like they weren't doing a good job?"

Mae shrugs. "We haven't heard from them in months. Just feels like no one cares enough to look anymore." He moves to the kitchen and she joins him. Together, they start opening cupboards. She watches him put the few mismatched plates, bowls, and utensils Inez owns into a box. Maybe he should be wrapping each one in newspaper, but she doesn't care enough to stop him. What does it matter, if Mae doesn't have a single lead in bringing her back?

"How did you meet her?" she asks him, hoping to be reminded of a not-missing version of Inez.

"She just showed up one day," he says, laughing. "She lost her keys and asked if she could use my fire escape to break into her apartment. It was such an Inez move, I'd soon find out. It wasn't the last time she'd lock herself out." He says it with such fondness that Mae has to wonder.

"You guys weren't . . . ?"

"No, no," he says, looking at her this time. "It wasn't anything like that. We were close but nothing ever happened between us."

She nods and busies her hands flipping through the cookbooks on the counter. But something isn't adding up. Inez is responsible. She isn't the type to lose her keys repeatedly. It's already strange that this is the messiest Mae has ever seen the apartment when Inez is the kind of person to wash the dishes at the end of every night. She double-checks the stove is off and the door is locked whenever they go anywhere. She carries Band-Aids and snacks in her too-heavy tote bag. She is prepared. Always. Mae is the forgetful one. The messy, chaotic one.

As if that isn't odd enough, Inez has never mentioned Dev. She's been living in this apartment since last winter. Mae has heard about her other friends, has even met most of them, but never Dev. Why would he say they were close if they weren't? Or why would Inez keep it from her if they were? If it's all true, if Inez has kept him from her for some inexplicable reason, then who knows the other little details that fill out Inez's life, the ones she's never shared. He is the living embodiment of the fact that Mae doesn't know everything about her sister.

The thought overwhelms her, and she finds herself walking away from him, creating what little distance she can in this small studio.

Across the room, Inez's desk is a teetering mountain. On the edge is the very dead succulent that Dev must have been trying to revive when she walked in. But it is no use. The cactus pads fall away at her touch, the soil dry and crumbling. She moves it aside and peruses the table. Papers cover every inch of the cheap wood. Mostly research articles with scribbled questions in the margins. There are thick stacks, barely stapled together. In yellow highlighter, Inez has marked up long passages about the history of the white painting. The intent behind the blank canvas. Mae flips through the manic research and finds that it's all the same, all analyzing one aspect or another of white paintings.

"Do you know anything about this?" she asks Dev, still staring at the papers.

"About what?" he says over his shoulder as he opens the fridge. A stench of rot and decay rolls out and almost knocks them both flat. Dev covers his nose with one hand and uses the other to dump everything into a waiting garbage bag.

"She has all these notes and articles about white paintings," she says once she can breathe again. "'A History of All-White Paintings.' 'Kazimir Malevich's *White on White*,'" she says, flipping through the stacks.

His brow furrows. "Maybe she was working on her thesis? That was due soon, I thought."

"Maybe." Mae feels a quick flash of guilt for not asking Inez what she planned to write about. Was she so caught up in her own life that she couldn't think to ask about one of the most important things in her sister's? She blinks the feeling away and focuses on the research. Dev is right. Inez would have been defending her thesis this summer, but something gnaws at Mae and she doesn't know why. The white paintings are as valid a thesis topic as any. Her frantic scrawl makes sense for someone on a deadline, and yet it feels like there is something Mae isn't seeing. She sighs and sits down in the wooden chair, pushing her knees against the desk and balancing the chair on its two back legs. The floorboards groan in rhythm beneath her weight. The sound brings her back to her own creaking floors back home, and suddenly it dawns on her. Mae jumps up, the chair clattering behind her.

"You know, when I offered to help," Dev says, "I didn't think I'd be doing all of this by myself."

She waves him off and makes her way to where Inez's bed is, the only space in the studio with a rug. Mae walks the length of it, one foot in front of the other, until she hears it again. The creak. Dev watches as Mae plops to the ground and lifts the edge of the rug back.

"What are you doing?"

"When we were kids, Inez loved to hide stuff from me."

She feels along the edge of the floorboards.

"I had a habit of reading her diary, so I couldn't blame her."

Their edges are smooth.

"But back home, beneath our rug, was a loose floorboard."

There, her nails find it, just the hint of a raised edge. With two fingers, she dislodges the piece of floor and it pops out with ease. She can't help the laugh that erupts from her.

"How did you—" His eyes are wide as he stares at the hole in the hardwood.

"If there wasn't one loose already, she would put one here herself, which means she chose where it would go. And she would have wanted it hidden but easily accessible. Old habits die hard. Why not have it covered by the edge of the rug too?"

He shakes his head in disbelief as Mae takes out her phone and shines the light inside the cramped space.

There, she finds a small notebook, tattered at the edges. Dust has collected atop its black cloth cover. She pulls it out, and from across the small room, she and Dev stare at each other, both frozen in place. It feels heavy in her hands. Significant.

Carefully, she opens it. Its frequent use is apparent in its full, barely legible pages.

Dev walks over to get a better look. "What is it?"

"I think," she says as she skims through it, "it's more of the same." She turns to the first page and finds that the notes, all dated like journal entries, begin four years ago, before any grad program or thesis research would, all about white paintings again and again. It's possible Inez has always been interested in these paintings and is using the grad program to delve deeper into them, but she's never mentioned this to Mae. Mae doesn't understand why Inez would keep it to herself if it was just a harmless fascination.

As she flips through the pages, the notes grow more frantic, less legible. A part of her is convinced this is something. That Inez is rushing, like she has stayed up late into the night trying to connect invisible dots. This feels like it is coming from a different place than academic obligation, somewhere personal and intimate. A place that has Inez hiding a journal in her floorboards instead of keeping it with the rest of her notes on her desk.

The rest of Mae wonders if *she's* the one connecting dots that aren't there, a desperate attempt to stoke what hope she has left.

Dev, using his cane as support, bends down to better read over her shoulder. But the handwriting only becomes increasingly difficult to make out, and both are straining to make sense of it. She flips to the last page and finds the date, December 5, 2023. The week Inez disappeared.

"I think this is the last thing she was working on," Mae says, and she breaks her own heart as this piece of her sister clicks into place. She can sense Dev studying her, but she doesn't tear her eyes away from the page, too afraid her face will betray her if given the chance. Near the bottom of the page is a messy sketch of a frame, a canvas, the dimensions scribbled around it. She's struck by the strangeness of its specificity. Everything else is about an idea, a concept. This is one painting. One piece.

She sets the notebook down on the bed, the edge of an idea teasing her as she scans the room. From here, she can see beneath the couch. Nothing but dust balls. She bends down to look under the bed and finds only loose socks and a wrinkled jacket. Just when she's ready to let the thought go, the glint of something shining against the lamplight catches her eye. Inez's closet, with its double doors slightly ajar, is right across from where Mae is sitting.

She crawls forward, pulls the doors open, and parts the clothes that hang there in half. There, she finds it. Behind her, she hears Dev's soft intake of breath.

A golden-framed painting takes up most of the closet. She leans forward and studies the ridges, the shadows they make. It isn't a fresh canvas, it's the kind Inez studied, the kind the articles talk about, the one her journal focuses in on. This is painted in thick white paint. Drips of it have collected and dried toward the bottom. On the top left corner, the edge has begun to peel. Mae has the sudden urge to grip it and pull it back, but she knows she'd be ruining it, whatever it is.

"This doesn't make sense," Mae says as Dev pulls it out into the light. He is gentle with its edges, careful of where he places his hands. He sets it down, and Mae can hear the weight of it as he places it against the bookcase. It is substantial, museum grade. "Why hide it in the back of her closet? Why put the journal in the floorboards?" She looks around the apartment, at the used books and secondhand furniture. Inez's thrift shop wardrobe. She eyes the couch they got off the street, the one they carried up a flight of stairs together and then spent the entire day deep cleaning. Inez doesn't even own a TV. The few times they stayed in, they had to watch movies on Inez's five-year-old laptop. The apartment itself is nicer than anything in it. And yet. Here is this massive painting fit for a museum.

"I don't know, Mae. I don't know why she has this." He studies the surface; his fingers trace the curves of the gold frame.

"What if this . . ." She trails off. She says it more to herself, but she looks up and finds his eyes on hers, waiting.

"What if this is all connected?" She can't help the desperate edge to her voice. She wonders if he hears it too.

They both look at the painting, willing it to spew out answers, but it just sits there, taking up most of Inez's wall. Dev looks back at her, his eyes reflecting the same questions she has in hers. He walks over to Inez's bed and picks up the journal, then skims through the entries.

"It's not much to go off of, but maybe," he says as he closes it. "Though the cops most likely looked into it already."

She shakes her head. "Everything is still here," she says, motioning toward the painting and scattered articles on the desk. "Which means no one took it as possible evidence. They haven't considered this. They just assumed it was all thesis research. Which, fair, it could be. But they never found the journal in the floorboards, and without it, there's nothing strange about any of this."

He doesn't argue. "So, what now?"

She shrugs. "Didn't even think I'd find this much."

After a while, they continue packing up the place as she wonders what this could mean, but it is all hypothetical. There is nowhere for it to lead. She packs the notebook along with the rest of the research into a box and throws Inez's clothes into a suitcase. They still smell like her jasmine perfume. Mae stops herself from inhaling too deeply, mostly to avoid any strange looks from Dev, and zips the suitcase closed.

The bathroom is a minefield of Inez remnants. Inside the small space, Mae finds it hard to breathe. Makeup and curly-hair products litter the sink. A towel lies crumpled on the floor. On the window ledge is a green glass vase of dried tulips, their thin stems weighed down by the petals. She picks up a tube of lipstick resting on the edge of the sink. *Fuzz* is written on the bottom. Inez was always so angry when she caught Mae putting on her makeup. She twists it open and slowly applies it, letting the soft reddish-brown color fill her lips. She tucks the tube of lipstick into her pocket. If Inez doesn't want Mae using her makeup, she is going to have to stop Mae herself. She grabs the makeup bag and half-used hair products and adds them to a half-filled box of books. What is the point of categories anymore? All she's doing is disrupting Inez's life. One day she will walk back in here and realize her shampoo is gone and her keys don't work. If Mae could buy the whole building, she would. Just so she wouldn't have to empty this bathroom and pack Inez's half-finished life into a box.

"Okay, we're done."

"What about the furniture?" he asks as he closes an over-stuffed box of coats and shoes.

"I'm not about to lug that downstairs, and none of it is going to fit in my dad's car. A donation company is coming for the rest. Take anything you want." She looks around the room. "Anything but the painting," she adds. She could leave it behind. Most likely, it will block the rearview mirror all the way home. And yet. The thought of leaving it behind is unfathomable. "I just—I don't know. I think she'll want it when she comes back."

He opens his mouth to say something, but she cannot have another person tell her *what if she doesn't*. She just can't. She lifts a box and leads the way out. He follows her to the car and they fill the trunk with two more trips' worth of boxes. She notices his limp is more pronounced without the cane, and he puts more weight on his right leg when he doesn't use it. Finally, they go back one last time to grab the painting. It's heavier than she expects, sturdy in her hands. She leads the way, walking backward until they reach the car, and once they've set it on the pavement, he disappears back inside to lock up behind them. Against the bright sun, beneath the corner where the paint has peeled, is a soft blue. She could swear there was no blue earlier, but it is clear as day now.

She reaches out to pull it farther back, but Dev's hand comes out of nowhere to stop her.

"I wouldn't do that if I were you."

"Why?"

"I mean, it could be priceless. You might ruin it." His brow is furrowed, his eyes more serious than she expects.

"Fair." Her hand slides past his and back to her side. She knows he's right. Still, she could swear it was white earlier.

"Ready?" he asks as he lifts the right side of the painting.

She nods, and they wedge it into the back seat with only a few inches to spare. But as Mae nudges it forward one more inch for good measure, she can feel something tucked in the back of the frame. She leans it forward against the front seats, and in the back is a business card.

"What is that?" Dev asks. She pulls it out and he leans forward to read over her shoulder. The smell of cedar and fresh laundry envelops her. In the light, they can see that the business card reads *Henry Hallward* in thick bold text. Beneath it, a slightly smaller *Fine Art*. There is a Boston address centered at the bottom. She trails her thumb against the raised lettering, the textured card stock stiff between her fingers.

"This must be where she got it from," Mae says to herself.

This.

This is the missing piece. The cops had disregarded this. If it's still here, it means they didn't even follow it down whatever rabbit hole it leads to.

But Inez.

Inez is what this leads to. Mae knows it.

Whatever is at the end of this, she must find it. Maybe Inez is out there searching for her own answers, or maybe something has happened to her because of that search. Maybe Mae is desperately grasping at answers that aren't there, seeing clues where they aren't. Some quiet, logical part of her knows that is possible too. But every other part of her is too loud to ignore. She doesn't care if she ends up being wrong. She just needs to know if she is right.

She pulls out her phone and does a quick Google search.

"What are you looking up?" he says. She tilts her phone so he can read the screen. Dev leans closer to make out the small text, and she can almost feel his chest against her back. She focuses on the phone. Henry Hallward doesn't have a website or number listed. Just the same address as the one on the card beneath a grainy photo of a storefront they can only assume to be a gallery.

"I'm going to go." She doesn't realize she's said it out loud until Dev speaks up.

"To Boston?" His eyes widen at the idea.

"Yeah," she says, turning around. His face is only an inch from hers. She glances at his lips before quickly looking away.

She can't tell if he notices her too-warm cheeks, but he takes a step back all the same.

"It's the only lead I have, Dev. She was researching the history of this painting. We know that much. Maybe I can follow it back. Maybe someone knows something, someone she came across while she was following this history too. Maybe if I can figure out how she got here, I can figure out where she is. The notebook in the floorboards. The painting in the closet. It has to mean something. Not to mention the fact that I can barely read her handwriting. I can't sit for months trying to decipher her scrawl when the answers might be out there if I just tried to find them." It isn't until she's decided she's going that she remembers her parents, realizes that she'll have to figure out what to tell them. She shoves the thought aside. She has time to figure it out.

He is silent for a moment, and she is convinced he is deciding if she is crazy or not.

"Can I come with you?"

Not at all what she thought he'd say. "What?"

"You're not the only one who cares about her. I want to help." He looks at her intently, almost pleading for her to let him come along.

She doesn't need him. She was ready to clean out the place herself, to find what everyone else missed, and she's ready to make this trip on her own too. But a thought comes, and it doesn't let her go. She thinks of Dev telling her how Inez lost her keys again and again, of not knowing about Dev until this morning, when she knows everyone else in Inez's life.

There are parts of Inez that only this boy with a perfect, square jawline carries, parts that seem to go against what Mae thought she knew. And no matter how much of Inez Mae knows, she does not have all of her. Dev is proof of that. Her curiosity feels like an insatiable thing, pulling her toward him. She needs to know what else Inez has kept from her, what she hadn't seen herself, and from who better than the boy with the answers. Plus, having him here has been a welcome surprise. Maybe it wouldn't be so bad to have the company. If Inez trusts him, she could too, she thinks.

And if she is being honest, she has no idea what she is doing.

"If you insist," she says.

Considering her entire plan is built around a clue that may or may not lead anywhere, she'll need all the help she can get.

Last Year

I nez knocks on the door, waiting for the boy she knows lives on the other side to appear. Eventually it swings open.

"Hi, I'm from next door. I locked myself out. Any way I can use your fire escape to break in?"

He laughs and steps aside. "Of course. Come in."

She walks past him and heads for his window, but once inside, she's in no rush to leave. "This place is beautiful. I have the studio version, and let me tell you, it looks nothing like this."

"Yeah, lucked out on this one. I'm Dev, by the way."

"Inez," she says, reaching forward to shake his hand. "Just moved in, so nice to have a friendly face around."

"Ah, welcome to the neighborhood, then."

There is a beat of silence between them, and so she takes that as her cue.

"See you around," she says, and with that, steps onto his fire escape and takes the two steps across to her window. She shoves it open and climbs inside. Back in her kitchen, she sets down her things. A backpack full of books. The headphones around her neck. And the apartment keys from her pocket.

Chapter 3

M ae's eyes are on the road, except for when stealing glances in Dev's direction. She can see the way his jaw clenches as his eyes focus on the road ahead, his fingers mindlessly pulling at the loose strands of his leather bracelet. She quickly turns back, and it's possible she is a little too close to the car in front of her, especially considering they are going seventy-three miles an hour. She switches to a different lane and slows down a bit. Dev's shoulders relax in response, only barely, but it's something. He slides the seat back a few inches to make more room for his long legs and starts shuffling through her music on the car screen, going through her playlist too fast to know if the song choices are any good. But his other hand grips the door handle so tight, Mae can see white knuckles against brown skin.

"Okay, what is it?"

"What makes you think there's anything?" he says, pausing on a Patsy Cline song and looking at her.

"We've been driving for ten minutes, and you haven't stopped fidgeting since you got in the car."

"Oh," he says, suddenly conscious of his body. He leans back into his seat and stays still. His fingers softly drum along to the song against his knee. There is silence for a few seconds. Only Patsy crooning about walking after midnight between them.

"You're just an intense driver."

"Is that another word for bad?"

He's quiet.

"I'm not though," she says too loudly not to come off as defensive.

"Mae, you almost rear-ended two cars in the last ten minutes. A truck swerved a lane over just to avoid you when you tried to merge onto the highway. *Intense* is generous."

She wants to argue. Who is he to think he can do better? But he isn't wrong. She hates driving. It isn't a secret. Even her own friends prefer to drive her everywhere just to avoid getting into a car that has Mae behind the wheel.

"You crash one car during a driver's test, and suddenly everyone thinks you're a liability." She rolls her eyes.

"What?"

"Nothing. Your anxiety can take a break for a few minutes. We need to stop for gas."

She switches two lanes over to make it to the exit in time, and she swears she can hear him audibly gulp.

She parks in front of a pump and they both get out.

"I got gas," Dev offers, and she doesn't argue.

"I'm going to get snacks," she says as she walks away. "Want anything?"

He shakes his head and leans against the side of the car,

keeping an eye on the pump. Inside the gas station, the AC blasts down on her bare arms. She walks down the aisle quickly, scouring the racks looking for anything remotely good. The shrill brightness of the fluorescents seems to pulse above her, and she's itching to be back on the road already. After months with no clue what had happened to Inez, here is a door, slightly ajar. She can feel the time slipping past her, wasted if not spent moving forward. She grabs an assortment of chips, one package of chocolate cookies, and two of the least toxic-waste-sounding energy drinks, and pays for her make-shift lunch at the register in cash.

Dev is staring at the car when she comes back, clearly avoiding going back in now that the tank is full and they have no other stops to make. She hates driving and he hates her driving. So it feels like a win-win when she throws her keys in his direction.

"I get full control of the music. Don't even think about asking to play a song." He grins and walks over to the driver's side, more than ready to take over.

They're quiet as Dev smoothly merges into traffic. He looks comfortable behind the wheel, seat already adjusted, mirrors appropriately tilted. If Mae didn't know better, she'd think it's his car she's gotten into. When he shifts in his seat, his eyes darting toward her, she realizes she's been studying him for a moment too long and looks away, keeping her eyes on the green rolling hills that line the road. She opens a bag of salt-and-vinegar chips and offers it to him without looking over. He takes a few and thanks her.

"What do you think we'll find in Boston?" he says around a mouthful.

What Mae would give to say *Inez* and believe it. "Nothing. A dead end is the most likely answer."

"Then why go?" He looks over at her for a second, his brow furrowed.

"Because there's a tiny chance I'm wrong, and I have nothing better to do than to prove myself wrong." She pauses for a moment, unsure how to explain that knowing this is a dead end is just as important as knowing it isn't one. She doesn't want to wonder about where this could lead. She needs to know. "She's out there, Dev. And I don't know if *there* is Boston, but I'm not going to stop until I figure that out, until I've confirmed every dead end is one, until she's back."

"I get it," he says, then after a bit adds, "Maybe she'll be there, waiting for us." Though Mae can tell the addition is for her sake, she doesn't care. The thought alone fills her heart.

"Maybe. Maybe she'll come back and laugh at what we're doing, say she took a spur-of-the-moment trip to Bali and lost track of time."

He laughs. "Or just moved and forgot to let us know."

She finally cracks a smile. She doesn't care that none of this makes sense, that Inez can't have moved because they were the ones who emptied her apartment an hour ago, that all her belongings are in the back. What does any of that matter when *what if* is stronger than logic? Hope is a hunter, and she is easy prey.

The conversation drifts, and they listen to Gin Wigmore on shuffle in comfortable silence. Eventually, she takes out her sketchbook and pencils and begins a rough sketch of the road ahead.

"Are you an artist?" he asks after a while.

He's glancing over at her sketchbook, and she has the sudden urge to hide it. It feels a step too far to call herself an artist. She looks down at the page and sighs. She can't even get the perspective right where the road meets the sky. "I dabble."

"That doesn't look like dabbling."

"It's kind of funny," she says, changing the subject, "that both Inez and I are interested in art. Sure, she's more interested in studying it than making it, but still."

He smiles. It doesn't quite reach his eyes.

"Okay. New rule. If we're going to drive all the way to Boston together, then no assuming she's dead."

"I didn't say anything!" he throws back, his eyebrows shooting up.

"You didn't have to. I could see it in your sad little smile. I don't need that kind of negativity. Either get on board that she's out there for us to find or get out."

He is quiet for a few seconds, possibly deliberating how he is going to get out when his car is a good hour behind them.

"With how you drive, I don't think you'd make it there without me."

She glares at him until he relents.

"Sorry, sorry. You're right."

"You're not just saying that because if you said no, I'd make you pull over on the side of the highway and walk all the way back to Brooklyn?"

He laughs, one hard laugh. "No, I mean it. She's out there. I know it."

"Okay," she says, squinting at him. She chooses to believe him, even if it's clear he is half humoring her.

He picks up the business card she placed in the cupholder between them. "Now, what do we have on this art dealer?" he says, his eyebrows comically serious.

She sets down her pencil and unlocks her phone, searches Henry Hallward and Boston again.

"Nothing. There's no website for a gallery, and he doesn't come up on social media either." She tries a few different variations of Google searches, but it is no use. "It seems intentional. Like he's got something against an online presence."

He shrugs. "A little strange for a business, but I guess not all that strange for a person."

"No way. It's even stranger for a person. No social for a business can be a gimmick. Like only those in the know can find it. But for a person? Just weird."

"I don't have any social media," he says after a beat. There's a hint of a smile on his face, already anticipating her reaction.

"None?" Is it too late to consider the possibility that she has gotten into a car with a serial killer? She has the sudden urge to look him up herself, almost to confirm what he's just said is true, but she realizes she doesn't even know his last name. Is Dev short for something?

"Why is that strange?"

"I—I don't know. It just is. Why don't you have any?"

"Takes up too much time, too much mental space. Think

about it. Really think about it. What's the point? What purpose does it serve?"

"For community, for checking in on your friends, for learning if you can trust strangers you agreed to go on road trips with?"

"You can do all that offline. And I doubt a picture of my morning cappuccino was going to answer that last one." He looks over as he says that and smirks. He has a dimple. She hadn't noticed that before.

"A cappuccino? What are you? Italian?" she teases him.

"It's a classic for a reason," he says a little too defensively. "And I would bet money you have an overly complicated drink order that, somewhere between your oat milk and your three pumps of lavender syrup, loses the entire point of coffee."

She doesn't deny it. "I refuse to let my lactose intolerance be used against me."

He smiles, and it's quiet between them. "You know you can ask me anything, right? Whatever you think you would have learned stalking me."

She turns in her seat to look at him. "Okay. Where are you from?"

He smiles but keep his eyes on the road. "Born in India, in Delhi, but my family moved to Vermont when I was a kid. You?"

"Pennsylvania. Parents came from Tunisia. Siblings?" She leaves no room for conversation.

His smile falters. "A brother. You?"

"Only Inez, but you knew that already."

"No, actually. Up until a few hours ago, I had no idea *you* existed. Who knows what else she kept from me."

"Probably a lot, if we're being honest," Mae says softly.

He rolls his eyes. "That makes me feel better." After a beat, he turns to her. "But really. I don't understand why she didn't mention you, why she kept that from me."

"I don't know, Dev." It stings, to know Inez never mentioned her, but she leaves the thought behind and moves on.

"What do you do?"

"I go to Columbia. Studying psychology. You?"

"Just graduated high school." She steamrolls ahead. "What are you going to do when you graduate?"

He shrugs. "I don't know. I just think it's interesting. Seems like enough for now. Learning about how our brains rule us."

"Fair."

"How about you?"

She doesn't know where to begin, how to tell him that as much as she wants—*needs*, says a voice in her head not so unlike Inez's—a year off, she doesn't want her family to fall apart. That a few weeks after Inez disappeared, she applied to the University of Pennsylvania and got in. Her family was so fragile then. Still is, really. One misstep and the whole thing will come tumbling down. She doesn't think what is left of her family can take it.

But getting in doesn't mean she has to go. She still has time to figure it out, she tells herself. She doesn't need to think about going to college or the fact that she has yet to decide on her plan for the fall.

Dev sneaks a look at her but she doesn't answer. She doesn't have much of one, and so she asks another question instead. "What's the worst thing you've ever done?"

He pauses, the smile frozen on his face like he hasn't decided if it should stay or not. "You think you would have learned that about me online?"

"Maybe not. But maybe all of that wouldn't have told me anything about you anyway." She studies his tense shoulders, his low voice, the way his eyes darken at the question. "Pretty bad, then, huh?" she ribs him, lightening the mood.

"No, I just—I don't know if I have an answer to give you," he says after a long pause.

"I think you do. But I'll respect your choice in keeping it to yourself," she says, letting it go. Yet she can't get the haunted look of his face out of her mind.

A small smile tugs at his lips until he releases it. "Thank you. How about you?" he says, turning it back on her.

"I think the worst thing I've done is only the worst because of everything that happened after." She doesn't know why she is so willing to say what she hasn't even said out loud before. Maybe it's that he feels temporary. A void she can throw things into before they disappear along with him. "There was a boy."

He laughs. "Isn't there always?"

She keeps going, ignoring the guilt twist in her. "There was a boy I was with the last time Inez called me, the night she went missing, I think. No one knows the exact day, but she didn't answer any of my calls or texts after that. I thought she was just busy, but someone she knew finally reported it when she stopped showing up to class, when they realized she wasn't home either."

There is so much Mae doesn't remember about the weeks

that followed. So much she let slip through. But not this. Every minute of that party is seared into her. She tells Dev all of it. Describes the throbbing bass of the music, the dark rooms lit by dim lamps. A late night made up of simpler times.

She still remembers Nico's minty breath as he shouted, "Do you want to go somewhere quieter?" into her ear, pulling her into focus.

She let out one quick laugh before she saw his face fall and realized he was serious. Nico was great, Mae knew this. A midfielder on the soccer team, a chiseled jaw she could cut sourdough on, and judging by how tight his T-shirt was, abs for days. But he had the personality of a sweet potato, and as fun as Mae believed it would be to sneak in a make-out session, his brother, who was watching them from his seat on the beer-stained couch, was who she couldn't stop thinking about. Even in the dim light of the living room, her eyes so easily found his.

For a second, she wondered if she could use this to her advantage. She could say yes, grab Nico's hand, lead him through the throng of dancing bodies, and make their way upstairs, all the while knowing Alec was watching them. She wanted him to see, wanted him to want her, but it felt too cruel to this boy with the big eyes and the bigger smile, to pit two brothers against each other when neither deserved it. She would find another way.

"I would, but," she said, checking her phone for the time, "it's getting late." She faked a yawn for good measure.

"Oh, okay. Maybe next time." He froze for a second. "I

mean—that's not what I meant. Not that anything was going to happen. I just—"

Mae smiled. "I know what you meant," she said, cutting him off. "Next time." She hugged him goodbye, and as much as she told herself not to, she snuck a glance over his shoulder at Alec.

His eyes were already on her as he sipped his beer slowly. He didn't look away.

She pulled herself away from them both and went to grab her coat from one of the guest rooms. The pile moved beneath her parka, and she left before whatever it was woke up. She walked toward the front door and a few people waved in her direction. One called out her name. She felt bad for a moment, not stopping, but quickly waved back and headed out. There were groups she hung out with, friends she enjoyed, but no one she felt bad enough leaving without saying goodbye to. There was always someone to see, people to surround herself with, but always kept at a distance. She didn't know why.

Outside, the air was cold as she dug around in her pockets looking for her car keys. It was just past midnight, and she knew she would be late getting home, but no use stressing about it now. Best to accept the fact that in ten minutes she would be sitting on the couch as her parents lectured her about missing curfew and her lack of respect.

"Mansour."

She turned around at the sound of her last name, and there was Alec in all his 6'2" glory. His curly hair was shorter than his brother's, tighter and cropped on the sides, and he wore a blue sweater that matched his eyes. There was a tear near the collar with the slightest sliver of kissable skin peeking through. He had his hands deep in his pockets, trying to keep the cold at bay.

"Can we talk?"

Her phone chose then to ring, and she silently cursed whoever it was for interrupting this soon-to-be perfect moment. She quickly checked to find Inez's name on the screen. Inez would have to wait.

"Yeah, for sure," Mae said as she ended the call.

He nodded toward her car and she unlocked it, leading the way. Inside, her car felt smaller than she ever remembered it being. He was so close, she barely had to lean forward to touch him. The smell of beer and cologne filled the small space, and she hoped it would burrow into the seats like it belonged there.

"I don't think you should lead my brother on. If you like him, great. But I don't think you do. I think you're just going to hurt him." He looked right at her as he said it. No wavering, no hesitation. "And I'm not sure you even care if you do."

She couldn't help her blushing cheeks. Okay, so this wasn't exactly the confession of his undying love she was hoping for.

"Alec, I didn't mean for—"

Her phone rang again. Inez. Again.

"Do you want to get that?"

"No, no. It's fine," she said, ending the call. She put her phone in the cupholder between them and focused on what he was saying. Which was difficult, given how his blue eyes seemed to glow in the dark.

"What makes you think I don't like Nico?"

"Do you?"

She paused, wondering if she should lie. But he was being honest, and she could do the same.

"Not in the way he'd like."

"Then tell him. Because he's already in too deep," he said, his voice low, smooth.

She considered him for a moment and made a decision. "What do I tell him? That I can't stop thinking about his brother?" Two could play at this game.

In the dim streetlight that lit up the car, she could see his jaw clench, could see his Adam's apple move as he swallowed. He sighed.

"Mae, he's my brother." But his eyes were still locked on hers, and they seemed to say something else.

"I know." She knew it had never been unrequited, that they had been circling each other for weeks now. Whatever this was, he felt it too. She leaned forward, a gamble when she didn't know if he would hurt his brother like this.

"We can't." And yet he looked at her lips as he said it.

"Okay."

And then he leaned in. She met him in the middle for a kiss that tasted bittersweet. There was a finality to it that she couldn't bring herself to mind. She would live in this moment, and in this moment, it would be enough. Her hand slid up his chest to rest at the edge of his torn collar, her thumb brushing the skin there. His lips were soft and urgent as his left hand cradled her jaw, the back of her neck.

Between them, her phone buzzed with a voicemail from Inez.

Dev reaches over the gearshift and squeezes her hand, shaking loose the memory's grip. "I'm sorry, Mae."

She freezes for half a second, surprised by the gesture. When she looks over, he seems surprised too, like his hand had moved without his knowing. He takes it away quickly, placing it firmly on the steering wheel.

"I'd planned to call her back the next day." She stares at the ceiling of the car, willing tears to stay put. "But I just let it ring, because I was with some boy. She texted me soon after. *Call me*, it said. By the time I did, she was gone."

They're both silent for a beat, letting the words settle between them.

"What did she say in the voicemail?"

She pulls it up and clicks play. The phone's Bluetooth is already connected to the car's speakers, and suddenly, Inez's voice surrounds them.

Hey, Mae, call me back. I need to show you something. Or tell you. I—I don't know. I've wanted to tell you for a while, but I didn't know how. I think I do now. Just—just call me back.

Her urgent voice vanishes, and the silence after feels louder somehow. Like it is a third passenger. Like she is sitting in the back seat, and they can believe it if only they don't turn around. But Mae does turn around, and all she sees is the white painting that takes up the entire seat.

"What do you think she meant?" Dev says into the silence.

His brow is furrowed, as if he's trying to decipher her words like he would a coded message.

Mae has memorized this voicemail, can recite it at will. She knows every pause and stammer as if she had left the voicemail herself.

"No idea," she says softly. "I don't know if it's connected. If someone didn't want her to tell me. Or if she left because of it. Or she was being dramatic and it was actually nothing at all." She closes her eyes. She won't let the tears come. Not now. "I don't know anything."

She opens them to see Dev's deep brown eyes flash to her, and for a moment, she can tell he wishes he could give her all the answers, but Inez has left them both in the dark. His eyes stay on the road, his hands to themselves. Mae's eyes turn to the trees and mile markers whipping past them on the turnpike. Mae only hopes that with every mile, they are getting closer. If not to Inez, then to the answers they need.

Chapter 4

The gallery is unassuming. A simple black storefront tucked between two much taller brick buildings. There are no business hours on the door. Just a large glass window with *Hallward Gallery* in crisp white lettering printed at the center.

"Do you know what you want to ask?"

"To be honest, this is as far as I've planned," she says, taking a deep breath. It hits her suddenly: She has no idea what she's doing.

Dev gives a wry smile and gets out of the car. "I guess we're winging this."

She glances at the painting resting against the back seat and pauses when she sees shifting shapes, a pressed pad of a palm, the outline of knuckles, the curve of long nails, half a dozen hands scattered across the stretched canvas. But then the setting sun shifts and the shadows dissipate. She can't make sense of them anymore. Doesn't know if they were there to begin with. She shakes it off and unbuckles her seatbelt.

"Grab the painting. Since we're asking him about it, I mean," she says, following Dev out.

He pauses as if he's considering arguing, but instead, he nods, puts his cane back, and slides the painting out of the back seat like it weighs nothing. The edge of his black short-sleeve button-up tightens around his bicep as he grips both sides of the frame. Mae looks away. What is she doing? She won't let a boy come in the way of her sister. Not again. This is a rescue mission, and here she is, losing focus, as if she hadn't learned her lesson the first time. Inez first. Cute boys with impressive biceps and adorable dimples later.

Inside, the gallery's ceilings are at least twenty feet high. Its hardwood floors and dark wallpaper complement the explosion of vivid paintings on the walls. All bold and beautiful and strange. At the center of the room stands a sculpture: a marble woman seems to be melting, drips of her collecting on the floor in matching marble. Mae tears her eyes away and finds what she's looking for.

Toward the back is a desk. A man in a bespoke navy suit she presumes to be Henry Hallward sits behind it peering over his round glasses as he types. He is older, late sixties perhaps, and is frowning at a wide, sleek monitor. At the sound of their footsteps, the man looks up. His eyes land on the painting and he smiles. It is a knowing smile, one you'd give an old friend you'd missed or thought you'd never see again.

"Well, this is a lovely surprise," he says. He is still looking at the painting, studying its canvas. Dev's fingers twitch around the gilded frame, and Mae is sure the gallery owner misses it.

"Looks like you two are familiar. I'm Mae, this is Dev. Your card was on the back of this painting, and we were hoping you could answer a few questions for us."

"Oh?" he says, finally looking at them. He pauses on Dev and his eyes narrow, like he's trying to place him. But he's too eager to get a closer look at the painting, and so he walks around to get a better view. Dev leans it against the desk and it towers over the man's monitor.

"Were you the one that sold it?"

"I was, yes. You know, this is the third time Delphine's white painting has come my way." Henry extends his hand toward the paint, reaching for it but not quite touching it. "It dates back to 1891 from little-known painter Delphine Lefroy. She disappeared soon after completing it. Rumors say she ran away with a lover, a woman that appeared in many of her paintings before this one. But the truth is irrelevant. Her absence created just the right amount of mystery around the painting that it's been studied again and again by a small but avid community." His eyes are lit with fervor, still glued to the painting. He runs a finger down its gilded edge, and it feels suddenly as if the painting has sighed.

"Why though?" she asks. A whole community? Was Inez part of that community? Why does anyone care that much about a white painting? She knows Inez had researched every facet of white paintings, but all Mae sees is a blank canvas. She studies it more closely. Would she have stopped had she seen it hung on this gallery's walls?

"Look at the movement of the brushstrokes. The deft layering. The raised texture. All invoking an examination of blank space. A dive into the void. It's quite remarkable. Ahead of its time, truly."

Dev raises a doubtful eyebrow, and Henry doesn't miss it.

"Do you disagree? Whether you approve or not, this is art. Many date the conceptualization of the white painting as art to Kazimir Malevich's 1918 painting *White on White*. But he was a man. Not many know it was Delphine who did it first decades previous in 1891 in *The White Expanse*."

"People see what you tell them," Dev says, visibly annoyed. "This talk of layering and texture, it's nonsense."

"Perhaps to the amateur eye," the man says.

Dev's ready to argue, his brows knitting together in frustration, but this is getting off track.

"You said this is the third time you've seen this. Who were the two you've sold it to?"

"That information is confidential, I'm afraid."

Mae doesn't know what to say to this. Should she beg? Flirt? Bribe? In the end, she goes with the truth.

"Here's the thing. My sister is missing." She takes out her phone and pulls up Inez's contact photo to show him. In it, Inez is laughing and Mae wants so badly to remember the joke. "It's very possible that this painting has something to do with that. I don't know how or why, but without those names, we're at a dead end. Please."

He glances at the photo, but there is no recognition in his face. He looks at Mae for a moment, deciding. "That won't be possible. Our clients' privacy is of the utmost importance."

"All we need is a name," Mae pleads. "Just somewhere to go

from here. Please." Her brown doe eyes are working overtime, but it doesn't seem to be working on him.

He shakes his head. "I'm sorry but I can't, not without a warrant, anyway. Now, unless there's anything else I can help you with . . ." He lets the sentence trail off, then stands and leaves to attend to someone else who has walked in.

Mae's jaw, her fists, are clenched. This can't be it. They didn't drive all this way just for some guy in a suit to tell them to go home. She refuses to accept that.

"Watch him," she says to Dev as she makes her way behind the desk. She is a girl on a mission. Nothing will stop her now.

"Watch him? What do you mean *watch him*? Mae, what are you doing?" His eyes widen as he realizes what she means.

"Getting those names."

"Goddamn it, Mae." He turns around, blocking her with his back and the painting so she can get what she needs. She quickly types *Delphine Lefroy* into the search bar of the gallery database, and one listing, *The White Expanse*, pops up. She clicks it and beneath it are two entries. Once to an Anthony Mason in Ottawa, Ontario, sold for ten thousand dollars in 2013, and once it came back to Henry Hallward a decade later, he sold it to an anonymous buyer, for fifteen thousand dollars. No name, no address. Just fifteen thousand dollars cash almost a year ago.

Inez was in New York then. Maybe *she* was the anonymous buyer, but she couldn't have spent fifteen thousand dollars on this, could she have? Mae thinks about Inez's bare apartment, how she can fit everything her sister owns, all thrifted and secondhand, into the back of the car. No. It doesn't make sense.

She wouldn't have had this kind of cash. And even if she did, she wouldn't have spent it on this. Someone else is the anonymous buyer. But then . . . how did it end up in Inez's apartment? Mae doesn't have enough pieces to put it together. For now, all they have is an Anthony Mason, so all they can do is follow the thread further back.

The desk is pristine. No paper in sight, and so she grabs a marker and writes out Anthony's address on her forearm. For a moment, she wonders if Inez had done the same thing. If she had scrawled Anthony's information onto her arm while Henry Hallward was busy. Maybe she had her own Dev as a lookout too. But before Mae can click away, she sees there is a note attached to the file. *Call Ravi*, it says. That's all. No number, no explanation. Just a name.

"Mae," Dev whispers over his shoulder. "Hurry," he singsongs. His broad shoulders are doing their best, but she can tell he is trying to make his body bigger, trying to take up more space to cover her.

"I'm done, I'm done. Calm down." She slides out from behind the desk and starts walking toward the door. Dev quickly follows suit, grabbing the painting and jogging to keep up with her.

"Thank you so much for your help, Henry."

She waves goodbye from across the room, but the second she does, she knows it is a mistake. He spots the writing on her arm instantly. His eyes narrow, and then flash to his desk as he quickly connects the dots. They both note the light from the now-turned-on monitor, the marker she left uncapped on his desk, the rolling chair no longer tucked in as it had been.

Henry turns to the back of the gallery and quickly signals toward a large man in a navy-blue polo, who meets Mae and Dev's panicked gazes with his own resolute one. He'd been so still when they arrived, Mae hadn't given him a second glance. Now his shoulders fight against the fabric of his shirt as he stands up from his chair and makes his way toward them, but before he's gone three steps, they book it out of there. They can hear his quick, heavy footsteps as he runs after them. But they have just enough of a head start for Mae to shove open the door for them both as Dev quickly limps out behind her, painting in hand. He slides it into the back seat and they jump in, the car already in drive before the doors even close.

An Interlude

1891

*T*hree young men stand feet away from a gleaming white painting. It sits atop a red oak easel in the center of the room, paint long since dried. To its left, a brush dipped in white has hardened since it was first swept across the smooth canvas. The gold foil of the frame shines in the beaming sunlight, untouched since it was first polished a month prior.

They have come a long way for this painting.

In the corner of the room, draped across a green velvet chair, is a woman with no name. Over millennia, she's been called many. None are hers. She watches them, basking in this quiet moment where none of them yet see her. She knows she can stretch this moment for as long as she likes, teasing it, pulling it apart until the boys turn, walk past her, and not once notice her.

But where is the fun in that?

She speaks out from the shadows. The boys turn to look for the voice, the body it belongs to, but the woman with no name is made of shadow. She is an absence.

Shadow wraps around her like a coiling snake, and when she walks toward them, they only sense a nearing darkness.

Until she sheds it like skin. A bare shoulder. A playful smirk. A sharp face you cannot look away from. The three boys watch in both fear and anticipation as she walks toward the painting, drapes an arm along the frame, and drags a finger across the contours of its surface. They do not notice the too-bright corners, the shadowless space beneath the easel. Do not see the way she pulls it all toward her, a thief made of night.

Their eyes follow her every move. Bodies tense. Shoulders taut. They do not know what to make of her. Only that she is what stands between them and what they want most.

Chapter 5

Dev and Mae spend the next twenty minutes glancing in the rearview mirror as they drive down random roads and turn onto side streets. Once they confirm they haven't been followed, they pull over. The adrenaline of racing out of there has quickly worn off. In its place is the small glimmer of hope that maybe they aren't at a dead end. Whoever this is might have the answers that Inez was looking for, might be able to shine a light on a part of this painting's past that can lead them to her. But for now, the long drive has caught up with them, and so they stop at the first restaurant once they know they're safe.

They step inside to find dim lighting, quiet chatter, and a young woman playing piano in the center of the room.

"Maybe we should find another place?" Dev says, hesitating. "I don't think we're dressed appropriately for this." Everyone inside is dressed impeccably, their hair voluminous and shiny, clothes ironed and tailored. It is not the sort of place you walk into on a whim.

But Mae is too tired, too hungry, to be bothered. She shakes her head. "All I've eaten today is a child-size bag of cookies. I dare her to turn us away." She approaches the hostess and Dev tentatively follows behind her.

"For two, please."

"Under what name?" the woman says as she looks up. Her smile is wide and full of teeth, the kind only a hostess who hasn't been worn down by the food industry just yet would have. The woman's smile dims, not quite reaching her eyes anymore, as she studies them. If Mae glances at a mirror, she will find that her hair is a disheveled mess, that her overalls are wrinkled. The stain near the strap feels more noticeable in a place like this. Mae can tell the woman knows there is no reservation. But she cannot find it in her to care.

"No reservation," Mae says simply.

The woman nods furiously as she checks the tablet in front of her. When she looks up, there seems to be an edge of panic in her eyes. She looks over their shoulders, and Mae's eyes follow to find a man in a black button-up in the window to the kitchen. The woman settles an internal debate and turns back to them. "You're in luck," she says, the smile barely hanging on now. "We just had a cancellation. Right this way." She grabs two menus and heads off, winding her way through the customers and waiters to a small, intimate table near the back. Mae can sense her relief that if she has to take them, she can at least tuck them away, out of sight from their usual affluent clientele, and possibly a manager who would have preferred they be turned away.

It's not until the hostess sets down both menus and lights a candle at the center of the table that Mae wonders if this was the right call to make. The candlelight flickers over Dev's features. Her eyes catch on his full lips. The shadows his long eyelashes make across his cheeks. The reflection of the flickering flame against his deep brown eyes that she now realizes are watching her too. His gaze is lengthy and heavy, and she feels every ounce of it.

She focuses on the menu, trying to clear her head. This isn't the time or the place, she reminds herself. Whatever ideas she is getting, she knows the responsible choice is to put a stop to them. Soon enough, he will go back to New York and she will go back home, regardless of how this ends. She hopes Ottawa will have answers. She doesn't know how long she can stretch this impromptu road trip; her parents still think she's in New York, and Dev surely has a life to return to. Mae skims the menu and can't help but notice the prices. Charging anything to her parents' emergency card isn't an option, unless she wants a frantic call from both of them demanding she come back home immediately. But she can't afford most of this, even with the cash she has on hand.

Eventually she settles on a shrimp linguini pasta. Moderately priced and most likely delicious. Dev orders the beef Wellington with truffle mashed potatoes. Her pasta is gone by his third bite.

"You eat like Inez," she says as she steals a forkful of mashed potatoes. "Her food is cold by the time she finishes."

He scoffs as he carves the tender, bleeding meat. "I think it's worth considering you're just an abnormally fast eater. That had to have been less than thirty seconds."

"Ah, but now I get to eat your food too. So, who's the real winner here?"

He rolls his eyes but moves his plate closer to her.

"So, where were you?"

"What?" he says around a mouthful.

"Earlier, you said you were away when Inez disappeared, that you'd just come back. Where were you coming back from?" she asks as she takes out her sketchbook.

"Oh. South America since December."

"December? Who randomly decides to go to South America for six months in the middle of the school year?"

"I do, I guess,"

"Ah, okay, I get it now. You come from money."

"I mean, define money," he says in a long drawl.

Of *course*. "Only people with money would say that."

He shrugs but doesn't correct her.

"Do your parents not care you dropped out for a semester?" she says as she starts to sketch his hand holding the steak knife. His fingers are long and delicate. Strong, but they move with a fluidity difficult to capture. She scribbles out the sketch and tries again.

"They're not really"—he pauses for a moment, looking for the right words—"in the picture."

"Ah, family drama. I am quite familiar."

"Inez didn't talk to her parents either, right?"

She looks up to see him studying the sketch. He glances at his hand, looking for the likeness.

"They haven't spoken in years. Since she was eighteen

and decided to go to NYU. They had certain . . . expectations. That she would stay close to home when she went to college. Didn't exactly work out that way." She moves on from the half-finished sketch of his hand and starts drawing Inez, her hand quickly flying across the page to keep up with her thoughts. "I've been lucky to have such a good relationship with her, even when she left."

He is silent as his eyes follow her pencil. The arch of her sister's nose, the stubborn edge to her sister's eyes.

"Are you and your brother close?" she asks.

"We . . . don't really talk."

"I'm sensing a pattern here, Dev."

He smiles, but it quickly strains into a grimace. "It's complicated," he says. "Which is to say I understand family estrangement, as much as I wish I didn't."

He takes one last bite and pushes his plate away.

"You ready? I don't think we can make it to Ottawa tonight, but we can check into a hotel and go first thing in the morning."

Her hand freezes midsketch. She feels her face warm at the word *hotel* but continues drawing, hoping he hasn't noticed the pause. "Yeah, let's," she says, nonchalant while feeling very chalant about it.

He offers to pay for the food, and she doesn't see the point in fighting him on it, given the fact that he has money to spare and her parents would panic the moment they saw a charge that big come from Massachusetts. She tucks the pencil into her pocket and follows him out, only wishing she'd ordered something more filling than her small plate of linguini.

"I should call my parents," she says once they are back in the car. She's avoided it long enough. It's getting late, and she knows they are expecting her home soon. Which means she needs to figure out some sort of excuse as to why that won't be happening. One they would believe.

He nods and waits for her to call, but by the time she realizes her Bluetooth is still connected to the car speakers, her mom has already answered.

"Mae, are you okay?" she says in Arabic.

"Yeah, I'm fine. I was just thinking maybe I could spend the night here?" Mae says, switching to Arabic.

Dev and Mae look at each other, waiting for her mother to respond.

"What do you mean *here*?"

"You know. Here, Inez's apartment. I just, I don't think I'm ready to say goodbye," she says, milking it. Which, obviously, is true, but she knows it's the chord she needs to strike.

"Oh, Mae." Her mom is quiet for a few seconds as Dev and Mae stare at each other. The car is still parked, and he quietly toys with the keys in his hand.

"She's not there. Not really, habibti. Come home. You'll feel better when it's behind you." Mae can feel her jaw clenching at her mother's words. She doesn't want to leave this behind her. Inez isn't meant to be left behind. She is somewhere out *there*, waiting for Mae. Dev studies her face, can surely feel the frustration coming off her in waves, and she knows he understands. He is here. He is missing Inez. And he is the only other person willing to do something about it.

"It's just for the night. There was more stuff than I realized, and I'm too tired to drive back now. I'll leave first thing in the morning. I promise."

Dev gives her a thumbs-up, approving of her lie, and she almost laughs out loud. She waits for her mom to decide, but the seconds stretch on.

"Okay," she sighs, like the decision has taken something out of her. "Get some rest. I want you to call me as soon as you're on the road."

"Thanks, Mom. I love you," Mae says with perhaps slightly too much enthusiasm for someone who is too tired to drive back home. They get off the call and Dev starts the car. He reverses out of the parking spot and starts maneuvering his way through the city.

She pulls out her sketchbook, taking advantage of the little light that is left.

"Wait," she says midstroke, thinking back to his approving thumbs-up and only now realizing she was speaking in Arabic. "Did you understand what I was saying? On the phone, I mean?" she asks in English.

He nods. "I'm a little rusty in the Tunisian dialect, but I got most of it, I think."

She stares at him, trying to process what he is saying. Most people can't even tell her where Tunisia is on a map, and here he is, able to differentiate Arabic dialects.

"Do you speak other languages?"

"A few. Hindi, Punjabi, Spanish, Japanese. I'm studying Russian right now but it's more difficult than I anticipated."

"Is this what a private school education gets you?"

He laughs. "I just like languages."

"You just named five and a half languages you're fluent in. You're past *like*."

He shrugs but doesn't say anything.

"How old are you?" she asks, exasperated.

He seems to tense, but it's gone before she can be sure. His fingers are light on the wheel, his face relaxed toward her. "Eighteen, give or take." He grins.

Mae shakes her head as she studies him. She's tempted to test him, but that would require her to know *any* of the other languages he's mentioned—and besides, why would anyone lie about something like that? It isn't hard to believe that with access to wealth, to private tutors and private jets, languages would come a little easier to people like Dev.

"A little genius," she says in Arabic.

He laughs, turning his eyes back to the road. But this new piece of Dev reminds her of how little she knows him, of how much of him she has yet to discover.

An Interlude

1918

*D*own a hallway, to the left, and up a stairwell is a room. There, the walls are adorned with mismatched paintings and glass displays full of strange artifacts. Treasures with puzzling pasts, or at least ones no one has been able to uncover just yet. It is difficult to find one unifying theme to the collection, but perplexing *comes as close as any word will.*

On the southeast wall hangs a white painting inside an ornate golden frame. Most museum visitors give it no mind, quickly moving on to stranger subjects. But two young men stand feet apart scrutinizing its mottled surface, its rough texture. There is purpose in its strokes, intent in its execution. Or so the placard to its right says. But the two know more about this painting than could ever fit on this small sign. If one studies the young men instead of the painting they stand across from, they will see a clenched jaw, listen closely for two racing heartbeats. They will see the shape of a fist in a pocket and wonder if there are fingernail marks against a palm to go with it.

A moment later one of them walks away without a word, and the other is left to watch as the crowd envelops him. It will be decades before they meet again.

Chapter 6

From Boston to Ottawa is nearly a seven-hour drive. And though Mae and Dev know this is where they need to go next, arriving on a stranger's doorstep at two in the morning to ask about a painting they may have owned a decade previous is less than ideal. And so they find a hotel in the middle of Boston and grab their things. In the parking structure, Dev locks the car and then locks it again, making sure the door doesn't budge when he tests the handle. When he seems satisfied that the painting and all of Inez's things are securely locked away, they make their way to the hotel.

The lobby is large yet intimate. Its high ceilings seem to go on and on in the dimly lit space of the entryway. The front desk is bookended with soft lamps on each side, and she follows Dev there. Mae doesn't argue when Dev offers to pay for their rooms, too focused on having to figure out what to tell her parents come morning when she's on her way to Ottawa instead of Benton, Pennsylvania. She knows she should have found a better lie, something that would have bought her a few days instead of a single night, but Mae doesn't doubt her mother would have shot that down faster than she could have asked. One night at a time. The morning will come, and Mae will figure out next steps then.

But it's easier said than done. Her stomach turns, already anxious at the thought of having to come up with another lie. Mae doesn't remember feeling this way before Inez's disappearance. She thinks fondly of late nights spent at parties or with friends, of lies that felt easy in her mouth. Ones her parents too easily swallowed up. But since December, the lies have grown sharp edges. She hates to admit that a sliver of their paranoia has taken hold of her, no matter how unreasonable. Mae knows that Inez's fate isn't this contagious thing, out there in search of her, but without knowing what happened to Inez, it's impossible to believe, with certainty, the thing her rational mind knows is true. For months, caution has been unwelcome company.

She starts to wonder if this trip is a good idea. If it's naive of her to think she can get to the bottom of this, can find Inez, by the time she has to go home tomorrow. Of course it's naive. There's so much she doesn't know, and yet she expected it all to open to her in a day, to flood her with all the answers to questions she has been asking since last December. But it isn't how these things work. She cannot force her way into answers, no matter how badly she needs them. And she does need them. She is willing to trust a boy she doesn't know for them, believing he wants to find Inez just as much as she does. But this entire eight-hour relationship is based on nothing but vague assurances. Who is this boy she is about to spend the night next door to?

Mae can sense herself spiraling, second-guessing every decision she's made in the past twelve hours.

The woman hands them each a key card and Mae follows Dev into the elevator. The black doors slide shut and the elevator begins its quick ascent to the twenty-third floor.

He gently taps her leg with his cane. "You okay?"

"Just . . . thinking," she says finally.

"About Inez?"

"Inez, my parents, how ridiculous this trip is to begin with. You."

"Me? What did I do?" he says, smiling.

She looks up to find his eyes on her, his dimple noticeable in the dim elevator light. For a moment, she loses her train of thought, but she blinks, and it comes back to her like a train through a tunnel.

"I don't know yet," she says. Before he can respond, the doors open to them and she steps out.

"Well, just let me know when you do," he says as they walk down the hall. He chuckles as he says it, but Mae can't tell if he's hurt that she doesn't trust him. They reach their rooms and he says good night before disappearing inside.

Mae steps in and throws her backpack on the crisply made king-size bed. She considers running a bath or settling beneath the covers. Turning on the TV and watching something mind-numbing until she falls asleep. But the last thing she wants to be is by herself in an empty room. She hasn't been alone with her thoughts since she got to Inez's apartment this morning, and now the quiet booms around her. A successful distraction is only wishful thinking. Nothing will keep her attention from Inez, from worrying over having to lie to her parents again, from falling into a loop about what tomorrow will bring, if anything.

Before she can change her mind, she finds herself knocking on Dev's door. She almost heads back to her room when he doesn't answer, but a few seconds later, he's standing at the open doorway, a confused look on his face.

"Mae," he says simply, like maybe he has uttered the word too late and she has appeared too soon.

"Do you want to go see if there's anything to do around here? I"—she hesitates here, unsure of how honest to be, and then—"I don't think I want to be alone right now."

It's all he needs to hear.

"Of course."

Dev grabs his cane, and the two make their way back down to the elevator.

They walk in silence through the lobby and out the front door. After hours of driving, being in the car is the last thing either of them wants, and so they opt to walk down the busy street. Eventually, they come across music pounding from a dimly lit bar. Suddenly, it's the only place Mae wants to be. She grabs his hand and pulls him into the crowd. He follows close behind her, cane in hand, and she knows if she were to stop walking, his body would collide into hers. She pushes the thought away and focuses on the bodies around her. The floor is sticky under her shoes, and she must force the crowd into parting around them, but eventually, she leads them to a table near the back. The place is warm and dark, but a few feet away a band is playing covers and people are dancing and it's so loud she can't think. What more could she want?

Mae turns to look at Dev, who is looking around him with a resigned expression on his face. "Do you want a drink?" he says, though it sounds like he's the one who needs one.

"I'm underage."

"Technically, so am I." He smirks and heads to the bar. She remembers drinking from a flask a friend had brought at home-coming. Something strong and bitter they had stolen from their parents. She doesn't remember liking it. If anything, all she really remembers is worrying if her parents could smell the two sips on her breath, if she would get a lecture about how haram drinking was and just how disappointed they were in her. But she is in a bar with no curfew miles from home, and she is feeling reckless. If this isn't the time for a drink, she doesn't know when would be.

The band pauses between songs, and the only sounds are the bassist tuning a guitar and the thrum of the people surrounding her. Dev comes back with two glasses in one hand, his other firmly on the cane.

"You don't seem like a whiskey girl," he says, setting them down on the table. "A gin and tonic." He pushes one toward her.

She takes a sip from her glass. The liquid burns almost like medicine all the way down, but once it settles, it feels warm in her stomach. Fuzzy almost. It's sweeter than she expects.

"Yeah, okay. That's not too bad."

He sighs in mock relief and watches the dance floor empty

between songs. "I don't even remember the last time I went dancing," he says, taking a sip of his whiskey.

"Inez never dragged you out for a night?" she says, thinking of all the long days spent walking the city only to leave before the night began.

He shakes his head. "She never really wanted to go out. We mostly ate too much food and watched too much TV together. Homebodies, the both of us."

Mae quirks her head, trying to fit the picture into her idea of Inez. It feels like an oddly shaped puzzle piece. The only days they spent in her apartment were when the weather forced them to. Inez is a different person to different people. She is learning that from Dev. But she can't help but wonder; did Inez feel guilty when they stayed in, pressured to show Mae a good time? Maybe she should have made it clearer that she was only there to see her sister, not the city. Inez could have moved anywhere, and Mae would have still been there just to see her.

Dev sits close to her at the small table, their knees touching, and Mae doesn't move. She welcomes the distraction. A part of her knows she should shift, twist away. But another, louder part wants so badly to lean into something fun and harmless, something that has nothing to do with a missing sister or a mysterious painting. She wants to flirt with a cute boy and have him look at her like she's all he's been thinking about. Where have the days of overwhelming crushes gone, and why can't she get them back? She decides that for one night, tonight, she will. This far from home, she can step off the pedestal her parents placed her on, the one that forces her to be the stable, reliable child, for their sake. For a single night, she will take every heavy worry that has indented itself onto her heart, set it down for a few hours, and just be eighteen again.

"Do you want to dance?" she asks him. But the band has started up again, and he can't hear her, only looks at her, confused. She takes out the pencil in her pocket and on the napkin between them writes *dance?*

She slides it toward him, and his eyes go wide for a second, surprised by the request.

Without waiting for him to answer, she gulps down the rest of her drink and pulls him onto the makeshift dance floor. He leaves the cane behind and lets her guide him to the edge of the churning bodies.

"I don't really dance," he says close to her ear.

"I don't either," she says as she moves her hips to the bass. The last time she danced was at a party last December. She skipped prom a few weeks ago, still not allowed to go out without her parents' supervision for anything but school, and feels the urge to make up for lost time.

She lets her hands land on his shoulders, releasing the tension from his body for him. Slowly, gently, he places his hands on her hips and moves along with the music, mirroring her body with his own. He takes small steps, the stiffness in his leg more pronounced without the cane. He smiles at her and she lets herself melt a little under his gaze.

The part of her that's saying *keep your hands away from him, don't slide them down his chest, don't step closer* is drowned out by the music, the heavy bass, and the vibrating speakers. There is only Mae in a city she's never been to with a boy she's just met.

She grabs his hand and twirls away, just as quickly coming back to land against his chest. He laughs, his dimples visible, and she has the sudden urge to kiss him. To wrap her arms around his shoulders, let her fingers play against the nape of his neck, his hair, and meet his smiling lips with her own.

She doesn't. Instead, she steps away, leaving space between their bodies.

"I think I need some air." She doesn't wait for him to respond, forcing her way through the crowd and toward the door. But the way he looked at her just before she left is already ingrained in her mind. His quick glance toward her lips and back to her eyes. The softening of his mouth. The firm grip of his hands on her waist. It isn't impossible to believe the same thought, want, had crossed both their minds.

She emerges from the crowd and into the arms of a heat wave that won't let go. With the warm breeze whipping through her hair, she can finally think clearly. It's one thing to dance with him, but that's as far as she can take this.

"You okay?" he asks once he escapes the crowd.

"It was just getting too warm in there." She turns to him, giving him her most convincing smile. She knows her cheeks are flushed, her heart pounding faster than it has any right to, but she hopes she can brush it off as the packed bar, the loud music.

He watches her for a moment. "Do you want to go for a walk?"

She nods and they head down the sidewalk together, an

arm's distance between them. She isn't sure if it's his doing or hers, but she keeps it.

It's quiet now, only the sound of occasional traffic, the shore in the distance, his rhythmic cane against the pavement. All of Mae's worries threaten to submerge her again, that quiet getting too loud, and she aches to fill it.

"What happened to your leg?" she asks, breaking the silence.

"An accident," he says, fidgeting with the edge of his leather bracelet. "The pain comes and goes, but it's just easier to manage with a cane." He rubs the worn silver metal of the rabbit-head handle. Its ears are peeled back, listening. The black metal of the snake beneath it catches the green neon sign and disappears again, only apparent in the light. She notes his ambiguous answer of *accident*, clearly made uncomfortable by the question, and decides not to ask for the gory details.

"How long have you had it?" she asks instead.

"Longer than I've been without it."

"Has anyone told you how vague you are?"

He smiles, bashful. "Sorry, I just don't think I'm all that interesting. You're not missing much."

"You just graduated high school, right?" he says, changing the subject. "What's the plan for the fall?"

She groans and throws her head back. "Not you too."

"What?" he says, laughing.

"If one more person asks me that, I'm going to walk right into that ocean."

"Technically that's the Massachusetts Bay, so . . ."

She rolls her eyes but decides to answer anyway. "What I

would like to do is take a year for myself, move to Chicago, and spend it drawing and visiting museums and *experiencing* new things and meeting new people instead of going to college without any idea of who I am or what I want." Mae feels a quiet thrill. She hasn't said this out loud before.

"But?"

"But my parents already disowned one daughter for going to college out of state. I don't think they can handle another one not going altogether."

"I mean, they would have to handle it, no?"

"You would think. But no. I swear, their marriage is hanging on by a thread as it is. Everything with Inez, it's been hard on them."

"On all of you," he reminds her as they take a left toward the water. They settle into a spot near the shore and Mae can already feel the sand inside her sneakers.

"Yeah, me too. But you get brown parents. It's different for us. I feel like this could be the thing that finally tears them apart." Logically she knows a gap year isn't the end of the world, but she also knows her parents would think otherwise. Her parents who, when Inez told them she was moving to New York, had redirected all their plans to Mae, their second and final chance to get it right.

"And yet, it's not on you to navigate that for them."

"Maybe you're right," she says, wanting to believe him. She leans back onto the sand, her elbows supporting her, and studies him. "Is that why you don't talk to your family anymore? Picked a path they didn't like?"

"Something like that," he says softly.

"Stole the family fortune and ran off in the middle of the night?" She nods understandingly. "Happens to the best of us."

He laughs, and it's a deep sound, a dam breaking open. "I knew you'd get it."

They sit in silence, all but for the soft sound of his cane scraping circles against sand.

"I hope you go," he says into the quiet. "To Chicago, I mean. I hope you find what you're looking for there."

"Thanks." And for a moment, she can almost see it. "I have an aunt I would stay with, and my cousin Mira moved there last fall. It's not like I would be alone. Maybe my parents would get on board eventually." But too quickly the moment passes, and the words feel flimsy in her mouth. "Have you been?"

"Once," he says after a while. "Never did go back." His lips pull to the right in a wince.

"How come?"

"Too much history there. Nothing I was interested in revisiting." He tugs at the edge of his leather bracelet, she notices. He does that when she asks him a question he doesn't want to answer.

"Sounds like there's a good story there."

"Just a long one," he says, smiling. It's a sad sort of smile, one she doesn't think is doing all that good of a job of hiding whatever is brewing below his surface.

"Come on, it's getting late. We should head back," he says, standing up. He offers her a hand.

She takes it, and both of them hold on a second longer

than they need to. She feels her face warm under his gaze, the weight of his hand in hers, his too-close body, and she lets go, turning away before he notices. They dust the sand off themselves and make their way back to the hotel.

By the time they reach their rooms, Mae is still too aware of his presence. Too focused on the little space between them. On his deep laugh and quick smile. She does not want to be attuned to any of it. Her mind flashes to an image from earlier tonight, sharp as if she had made it herself. The candlelight reflecting off Dev's eyes. Him meeting her lingering gaze with his own. The hint of a smirk as the flame flickered between them. She feels the heat of it all over again and, with it, a surge of frustration that the only place her mind wants to frequent, aside from Inez, is Dev.

She slides the key card against her door and mumbles good night. She doesn't wait for him to respond, only closes the door behind her and leaves a confused Dev on the other side. She can't even blame him. Mae has, after all, spent the night giving them both whiplash; she'd enjoy his company a little too much and then shove him aside with a vow not to let boys be a distraction, only to break it just as quickly.

Not until she's alone in her room does she realize she should have taken some of Inez's clothes to sleep in. But she hadn't thought that far ahead, and now the overalls she's been wearing all day will have to double as pajamas.

She takes off her shoes and resigns herself to turning on the TV to a sitcom she knows will not be enough to soothe her, and settles into bed. In the lamplight, she flips to an empty page in her sketchbook and tries to get rid of the leftover energy with some mindless drawing. But it doesn't seem to work because after an episode of *New Girl*, the page is only a puzzle made of Dev. A dimple. A hand. A neck.

Even when she puts it away, all she does is twist and turn all night, her mind leaping from Dev to Inez to her parents and back again.

When she finally falls asleep, she spends the night running through a dream, surrounded by a green hedged maze with walls twenty feet high. She runs past Inez and looks back in agony, willing her limbs to stop, to go back.

They don't.

They force her through a labyrinth of answers she cannot see the end of. Henry Hallward's face appears and vanishes behind her, and again she doesn't stop. She cuts through corners, down narrow paths, and at the end of a lane is a man with his back to her. *Anthony Mason*, the dream tells her. She does not doubt it. He stands still, waiting, and so she runs faster toward him, but when he's mere feet away, he turns down a corner and disappears.

Mae runs after him. When she makes it around the bend, he's gone. In his place stands Dev. Only when she rams right into him does her body let her stop. He smiles down at her, his hands gripping her shoulders to steady her, and says, "Mae." Like he had summoned her here himself. She tears her eyes away from his to find the painting resting against the hedge. Except here, it begins to shift. Its canvas stretches as hands, so many hands, push against the surface. Their knuckles are white as they grip the fragile frame from the inside out. Mae wants to look away, wants to run, but she can't. Her body is still. Her eyes are glued to the painting, this time to its center as a face begins to form. A chin, a nose, an open mouth. It's only until the hair appears that she realizes she's staring at Inez. At some twisted version of her trapped beneath stretched canvas. Her mouth is frozen in a silent scream and all Mae can do is stand there and watch.

An Interlude

1937

*I*n the cargo hold of a ship lies a box carrying a painting. The space is damp and cramped, and inside the crate, the mahogany wood beneath the gold leaf begins to soften, the frame fragile now. The canvas, with its rolling waves of white paint and curling corner, considerably more curved than when it was packed away, sits in darkness. All but for a crack in the crate that lets a slip of light shine through.

The box jostles back and forth with the tide as it makes its way down the Mississippi River.

Chapter 7

JULY 17, 2024 10:45 A.M.

When Mae arrives in the lobby, she's already made the decision to keep a safe distance from Dev. As much as a cramped car will allow, anyway. There may be no way to truly escape his presence, but she *can* quell whatever is brewing inside of her.

The elevator doors open and a tired Dev steps out.

"Morning," he says, and all she gives back is a tight-lipped smile. When he reaches her, she sidesteps him and heads for the desk to check out.

They walk to the car in silence, and Mae can feel the tension she's creating. So be it. She wills herself to ignore every unnecessary Dev thought that flies into her head.

He buckles his seat belt and waits for her to do the same before they start the journey to Ottawa. She feels her phone vibrate and knows it's her mom calling for an update before she even checks. She glances at Dev and ends the call, vowing to call her back when she can muster the energy for another lie. For now she's got enough on her mind. After a few minutes on the road, Mae already can't stand the quiet and connects her playlist to the car speakers.

"Sleep okay?" he finally asks.

"Yeah."

"Cool," he mumbles. "Cool cool cool."

For the next few hours, she focuses on sketching and is pleased to find that not a single part of Dev makes it onto the page. Eventually, when he suggests they stop for lunch, she insists they use a drive-thru to not waste any time. If she doesn't have to sit across from him and share a meal, she won't. They grab burgers and fries, a drink each, and as they get back on the highway, she steals glances his way, tasting just the slightest tinge of guilt with each fry as he struggles to keep the car straight with one hand and eat a burger, sauce dripping on his black jeans, a tomato slice slipping out, with the other. The kind thing would be to feed him a fry so he can focus on driving. What's a fry between friends? But they aren't friends, and so she resists, and a frazzled Dev ends up in the wrong lane and misses their exit twice.

Mae pretends not to notice as he swears to himself and quietly disconnects her phone from the speakers. She considers which parent to call for a second. She called her mom yesterday and may have used all the good will she has with her for this trip. She taps her dad's photo and waits for him to pick up.

"Mae?"

"How are you?" she says, switching to Arabic.

"How am I? Your mom called you hours ago and you never answered. How do you think?"

She nods, already off to a bad start. "You're right. I'm sorry. I was just busy packing and lost track of time."

"Are you done, then? On your way?"

"About that," she says, letting the words hang between them.

He sighs but doesn't say anything.

"I just need one more day here! You were talking about how you and Mom have spent so much money on this apartment, I just wanted to try to get some of that back for you. I sold the couch and bed online, and the woman who plans to pick them up can't make it until the morning. I'll get on the road the second she's done, I promise!" With her poorly prepared case over, she waits for his verdict.

"You don't have to do that, Mae." She hears that usual discomfort in his voice when money comes up around her. "We'll be okay."

"I know. But I want to help. Let me do this for you."

Just when she thinks he's about to demand she come home right now, literally impossible when she's about to cross the border into Canada, he grants her request.

"Tomorrow morning. The second you're done. Okay?"

"Okay!" she says too enthusiastically. "And you'll tell Mom?" she quickly adds.

He chuckles. "Yes, I'll tell Mom."

They say goodbye and Mae connects her phone back to the speakers.

"Everything okay?" Dev asks.

"Got the okay to stay another day, but you knew that already," she says in Arabic.

He smiles, and it unfortunately eases something in Mae. They listen to the music the rest of the way, a compilation of Hozier, George Ezra, and Alabama Shakes. She doesn't ask if he has any requests, but he nods his head along to a few songs, so she figures it's fine.

Around seven thirty, Dev takes the final exit, and three turns later, the two find themselves slowly driving down a long private road with large sycamore trees lining both sides. Their branches are long and thick and bend to meet at the middle, blocking most of the late summer sun.

At the end of the path, a house appears. Though words like *villa, mansion, estate* are all closer to the truth.

"Holy shit," Mae whispers, and the words seem to diffuse a bit of the tension in the air. They glance at each other and back to the behemoth of a house.

Four white marble columns rise to the second floor and then the third, meeting the dark, sloped roof. Long, dark windows take up much of the stone facade. The rest is made up of large white panels. It's grand and pretentious in the way only too much money can be. Set back from the road, a circular driveway lines scenic landscaping that refuses to wither in the summer heat, tulips with their upturned petals and stiff stems, as if they'd ever give in to something as pedestrian as the weather.

Dev parks and they just sit for a moment, taking in the obscene display of wealth.

"So . . . looks like yours, or not enough columns?"

He rolls his eyes, but she notes his lack of denial. She turns her attention back to the estate. Mae doesn't doubt that whoever lives here is more than willing to drop ten thousand dollars on a painting that looks like a blank canvas, no matter what Henry Hallward saw in it.

"Do we know what we're asking, or are we doing what we do best and winging it?" he asks.

Mae makes incredibly awkward finger guns at him that she immediately regrets. "I think you know."

They get out and make their way to the glass double door. Dev glances over his shoulder at the painting in the back seat, as if nervous to leave it behind.

"We don't need it. How many blank paintings have these people bought that they won't know which one we're talking about?"

Still, as he nods and rings the doorbell, she grabs the keys from his hand. She clicks the lock button and pockets them, the car sounding off two loud beeps.

He looks at her with a raised eyebrow and she shrugs.

"Better safe than—" The door opens, cutting her off.

A woman in her late fifties answers the door. They haven't said a word yet, but she already looks annoyed they are there.

"Yes?"

"Hi, is Anthony Mason home?"

"You're a decade too late, sweetie. Anthony is long gone."

Dev and Mae look at each other with raised eyebrows.

"Oh. Well, I'm Mae, this is Dev. We just had a few questions for him—but maybe you can help us."

She looks at them for a long while before sighing. "Ava."

Ava grabs the drink she had placed on a small table near the door and turns away, leaving it open behind her. Mae looks at Dev, but he just shrugs, as bewildered as she is. They follow her in, and Mae, last in this small procession, struggles to shut the heavy door behind them. Understandable, given that it's twice her height. She runs down the unnecessarily long corridor and catches up to Dev in the living room. There, marble floors and white walls fill the space. Everything from the equally bright white couch to the fluffy white rug is pristine and impossibly clean. It is hard to believe anyone truly lives here.

Ava sinks into the long white sofa that sits at the end of the room, the red wine in her glass sloshing dangerously to the side. She trades her glass for her phone, and the two wait as she types something into it.

"We were wonde—" Mae begins, but Ava holds up one perfectly manicured finger and continues typing with the other hand, clearly in no rush to address them.

"So, what did Anthony do to you?" she says, finally setting the phone down and raising the glass to her lips again.

They look at each other, perplexed at this strange woman with her sloshing wine and devil-may-care attitude. Mae doesn't know where to start, so she starts with the obvious.

"He bought a white painting in a gold frame years ago. Do you remember it?"

Ava rolls her eyes. "And here I thought I was rid of that monstrosity. Almost twenty years with that man and I still couldn't understand his taste."

"Are you his wife?" Mae asks, and the question twists the woman's mouth into a smirk. A cruel slash along her face.

"I was, once, yes." She pauses to take a sip of her wine. "But that was a long time ago."

"What happened?" Dev asks.

"He left. I don't know much more than that. One day he was here, and the next, gone."

"Do you mean he disappeared? Is Anthony missing?" Mae asks, and the question feels too hopeful on her tongue, too heavy.

"I don't know that it counts as missing if you leave with your mistress. Or mister? Anthony didn't discriminate when it came to his affairs. But he was a serial cheater if I ever met one. He would focus in on someone, then grow distant, and fall for anyone that eventually reciprocated the attention. It would fizzle. It would repeat. It was a cycle. I didn't mind." She pauses, her eyes darting between them. "Maybe I should have known, I was one of them once." She laughs, but it sounds false. She finishes the wine in a large gulp, a small trickle falling down the side of her lips, then wipes her mouth with the back of her hand. "But there were certain sacrifices I knew I'd have to make for this life." She gestures around her as if this living room with its pristine white rug and gleaming black marble fireplace are the only explanation necessary.

"Anyway, I don't know where the hell he's gone or who he's with now, and I'm not interested in finding out. What, does he owe you money or something?"

Mae's heart gives a lurch. Maybe this means there are others. Maybe Ava would rather believe he left her for someone else than never know where he is or why he left. Could there be more to the story than Ava is willing to admit, even to herself?

But deep down, Mae knows it is a leap to think Inez isn't the only missing person connected to this painting. She is latching on to any possibility, any lead, valid or not.

"Do you know why he bought the painting?" Mae asks, hoping that Anthony was as riveted by the painting's history as Inez, that he wasn't just an impulsive man with too much money. Her eyes flit around the room as she looks for anything she may have missed when she first walked in. She is running out of questions, desperate for any sort of clue. Something she could hold on to instead of wonder about. Crumbs would be a welcome reprieve.

Ava laughs one hard laugh; it erupts from her mouth like it snuck out. "I don't know why he did anything, least of all buy a particular painting. I just know it was his favorite piece, and I was happy to see it go. I held on to it for years, too many years, but eventually realized it just fueled my anger for Anthony." She pauses to finish the rest of her wine and stretches along the length of the couch to set the glass down on the end table. Mae hadn't even seen her refill it. "He would stare at that thing for hours, mesmerized by the white expanse of it all. I didn't understand it, any of it. Every time I walked past it, he was all I could see. It took a decade of therapy to learn anger was a comfort, familiar, that I couldn't put him behind me until this was too."

The three sit in silence for a moment, letting it settle between them.

"Has this woman ever come to see you? To ask you similar questions maybe?" Mae says as she takes out her phone and pulls up a picture of Inez smiling into the camera, hair wild in the wind. She sits on the grass atop a checkered blanket. There is a half-finished sandwich by her side. Mae closes her eyes, burning suddenly at the memory.

The woman studies the screen.

"No, I'm sorry. I don't know her." Ava shakes her head, bringing Mae back. As she hands the phone over, the sound of the doorbell turns all of their heads toward the door.

"Oh great, he's here," she says with a smile. "Turns out we have a mutual friend." And with that, Ava leaves to answer the door, making the trek down her long entryway. Through the sheer curtains atop the glass paneling to the right of the front door, Mae can barely make out a face, but when she turns to Dev, she sees all the color has drained from his. His eyes are trained on the opaque glass, on the shape of the man who stands on the other side.

"Hey," she whispers, nudging him. "You good?"

"Mae," he says as he tears his eyes away from the door. "Do you trust me?"

"Considering I just met you yesterday, not really, no," she says. She tries to read his face, to look for the humor, the joke, but his eyes are large and serious, and they are trained on hers.

"We have to go. Please," he begs, and she nods slowly.

"You know you're going to have to explain why you're act-ing like you just saw a ghost, right?"

"Later, I promise." Dev grabs his cane and takes her hand, leading her to the glass door on their left that opens to the back-yard. Even now, as she slips on the marble floor while rushing behind him, she can't help but notice how soft and firm his hand is enclosed around hers. His skin is a few shades darker than hers, warm in tone and in temperature. Her heart beats a little faster, but she isn't sure if it's because they're sneaking out the back door of this woman's house or because of who she's doing it with.

They're out before Ava has even made it to the front door. Dev leaves the back door open behind them, and they run along the side of the house. He reaches the edge and comes to a stop when he hears Ava opening the door to the man on the other side. Mae collides into Dev, and he reaches back to steady her against the stone wall, gentle but firm. He leaves an inch of space between their bodies, and Mae feels the empty space like it is a tangible thing separating them. His lips are slightly parted, and he's focused on listening to the hurried conversation between the man and Ava.

Dev looks down at Mae, and she quickly looks up from his mouth to meet his eyes. One of his hands rests on the rabbit-head cane, the other at her waist to stop her from going any farther. Dev is distracted as he waits for the man to step inside, and she wonders if she's the only one who has other things on her mind. At the sound of the door shutting, she opens her mouth to ask if the coast is clear, but he takes the hand at her waist and raises a finger to his lips. His eyes are pleading, panicked. Through the cracked window over Mae's shoulder, Ava's voice drifts out, and he closes the distance between them to avoid being seen, his thumb grazing her hip. Her breath catches as she feels his pulse racing alongside hers.

Eventually, finally, quickly, he takes her hand again and they sprint to the car. He runs ahead of her to the driver's side, and it's only then she realizes he had quietly slipped his hand into her pocket and taken back the keys. Mae doesn't know why she's running, only that Dev needs her to and so she does. She jumps in as he turns on the car, and in that moment, the front door whips open. A boy grips the door handle as he looks back at her, and she wonders if it's just the stress of the moment, the adrenaline playing tricks on her eyes. Her mouth opens, just the tiniest bit, as she tries to process what she's seeing.

Feet away at the open doorway is a boy who is Dev but isn't. His hair is buzzed and the eyes are different, sure, but it's the same strong nose, the same sharp jaw. She looks back at Dev to make sure she's not hallucinating and sees that the panic on his face has turned to anger. He puts the car in drive and speeds past the boy, who watches them leave with the poised stillness of a serpent. They are close enough that she can see his jaw is clenched, his chest rising and falling from running back to the door. His right hand is a fist at his side. But no matter. Dev turns down the circular drive. He maneuvers around the other boy's green truck, which hadn't been there before, and makes his way back to the road.

The boy who is and isn't Dev watches as the car disappears around the bend.

Chapter 8

In the shadows of the woods lives a woman with no name. If one knows what to look for, they can separate her from the trees. Can pick out branches from limbs and hair from leaves. They can look into the darkness and see her looking back, two onyx eyes formidable in their ferocity. But no one knows to look and so no one sees the woman with no name.

When she ventures out of the woods, she spills into spaces like water. Falls through fingers and away from curious eyes before anyone can make sense of her. Unless, that is, she wants them to. Unless she sets her gaze on them and does not let go. It is desire that draws her out, a want as staggering as her own imposing power. Tonight, she can sense it and is almost overwhelmed by it, inundated by its sheer force.

Dev Sharma is fortunate enough to be seen. Though *fortunate* is a strong word and, depending on who you ask, entirely inaccurate. You see, the woman with no name knows much more of you than you know of her. In Dev she sees desperation.

A simmering kind that lives just beneath his skin.

A well of yearning so deep, she cannot see its bottom.

In a way, their crossing paths were inevitable, fated. As powerful as she was, she was so intensely drawn to his infinite well of want that she chose him as much as a moth can choose to turn toward flame.

The woman with no name steps out of the dark, and there, at the edge of a pendulum, her eyes meet Dev's.

He hears the voice first.

"You want something."

Dev turns to see a woman made of shadows. He blinks and she steps forward into the moonlight. He is unsure if he is the target of this woman's attention. But he walks home alone at night along the edge of the Wildwood, and there isn't a soul but his for miles. He notes her bare feet, the white cloud of hair that surrounds her. It wraps around her shoulders and ends at her waist, one soft, hazy storm as if she has meticulously brushed out every curl. But it's her black, dark-as-night eyes that entrance him, rooting him in place. He couldn't escape her if he tried. It will take him a lifetime to learn that, to know this moment was inevitable.

He opens his mouth, though he does not know what to say, only continues to take her in; but she is an ocean, and he is a cup. He will never truly fathom her. She steps closer, close enough to touch, and he understands she is more creature than human. More wild than woman. He knows, the moment their eyes lock, whatever she and he are made of, they are not the same.

"You want something," she repeats. Her voice is low, smooth, and it wafts in the air, so he can't quite make out the source, even though the woman stands before him. She leans in closer, enough that he can feel her cold breath against his cheek, and whispers, "Escape."

His eyes go wide, as if she has pressed her finger to a bruise, and he is afraid to admit he understands.

"What you seek lies beyond this town. Beyond its borders and all they hold. It is a painting made of want and there it lies in wait. Find Delphine Lefroy. Find her painting, and what you seek most shall find you."

He does not know what else to do but nod.

"Be warned," she adds as she drifts around him. "It will give, yes, but only as much as it takes."

Dev does not think to question her. He takes this as fact, as if he's known it all along. It is not until later, when she's vanished into the woods, that he wonders if this was all one lucid, walking dream. If she ever existed to begin with. But existence is a fickle thing, and Dev does not yet understand he is asking the wrong questions.

The woman with no name is made of shadows once again, her silhouette barely perceptible in the darkness. He blinks, and the only trace left of her is the chill down his spine from her cold breath against his cheek.

Chapter 9

"That's it? You're not going to explain?" Mae asks. Again. He drives in silence, avoiding any questions he isn't in the mood to answer, which, so far, has been all of them.

"You're really not going to tell me why we ran out of there? Or who that guy was? Or where we're even going?"

"I told you. I didn't trust Ava. She was up to something and I had a bad feeling about it. I trusted my gut and got us out of there."

"And I told you I don't believe you. There's something else. You know more than you're letting on."

She is met with more silence.

"Fine. I can make my own guesses. Clearly, the guy at the door is the brother you mentioned, the one you don't talk to. If you want to tell me I'm wrong, you can, but it's unlikely I'll believe you."

His jaw clenches in the dimming light, and she takes that as a sign she's right so far.

"You owe him money."

Here his shoulders relax. Okay, Mae thinks, so she's off base.

"You killed his dog. You burned his house down. You slept with his girlfriend. No. His boyfriend," Mae says in mock horror. "How could you?"

He smiles before he catches himself a second too late.

"I promise I want to tell you, Mae. I do. But I just—I can't. For right now, I need you to trust that I have my reasons and they would be valid had I said them out loud."

She isn't sure what to say to that. It is honesty she is asking for, and here he is being as honest as he is capable of. It just isn't enough. Mae doesn't care about the reasons he's withholding the truth. All she cares about is finding Inez, and here he is taking her farther away from answers Ava could have had, answers that his brother, who she's now realizing must be connected to all this somehow, has. His showing up was as good of a lead as she was going to get, and Dev robbed her of where it would have taken them.

She's been patient, she's tried to keep the conversation light, but he doesn't deserve her generosity. This boy who she's trusted too easily. She studies his profile: the sharp slope of his nose, the soft dip of his mouth. It dawns on her that she's let her shallow feelings, his lingering gaze and easy smile, distract her from the only thing that matters. Finding her sister, the only person she's ever really cared for, that ever saw her truly. Inez. Why had she so easily believed that he wanted the same thing? Is it possible that he is here only to keep her from the truth? Whatever it is?

"It's late, I'm just driving to a motel for the night until we can figure out what to do next. Is that okay?" He tears his eyes away from the road and glances at her, waiting for her approval. His eyes are kind and pleading and she wants so badly to trust them. To trust him. But the voice in her head is too loud now. She nods and he turns back to the road just in time to make the exit he needs.

Two hours after they floor it out of Ava's, they find themselves in a motel just outside Montreal. It's set close to the road and the parking lot is full. It's not exactly what she expects. After all, Dev has the money—they could have been in another hotel calling room service. But instead she finds herself staring at a run-down two-story building with a flickering VACANCY sign in the office window. Not exactly the Ritz.

"I'll go get us two rooms," Dev says as he puts the car in park. "Do you want to grab your things? Inez might have clothes you can borrow for the night." Mae nods, noting his use of *borrow* instead of *have*. *It is only a matter of time before she comes back for her things*, he seems to say. This morning she would have thought it sweet, would have appreciated the distinction, but now she wonders if he's simply clever enough to use the right words, to make her think he's on her side. He heads inside, and she grabs her backpack before opening the trunk to look through the poorly packed boxes and suitcases.

A part of Mae breaks in two as she opens a suitcase full of Inez's clothes. But she shoves that piece deeper, knowing that feelings like these don't align with the reality she has created for herself, one that has her *borrowing* her sister's things. She closes her eyes. Takes a deep breath, and it is a mistake. The scent of Inez's perfume fills her nostrils, and all she wants to do is let the rest of her fall apart too.

"You okay?"

She hears his voice over her shoulder, and it feels too heavy to have to lie to herself *and* someone else. She finds it in her to nod but doesn't turn around, too scared her face will betray her if she does. But she can feel him close and knows she isn't fooling anyone.

"I'm sorry, Mae."

"For what?" she says, finally turning around. His eyes are large and sad and full of pity, she can see it.

"That you feel like this. That I can't do anything to fix it. That I . . ." His words trail off but he doesn't say anything else. Only clears his throat and looks away.

She doesn't know what to do with that. She can tell he means it. It doesn't change anything. She is of single focus now. "Are we all set with the rooms?" she says, busying her hands by taking a few things at random from the open suitcase.

"Change of plans. They're booked for the night. We got the last room."

Mae laughs one quick laugh, suddenly reimagining the entire night in a way she hadn't expected. Of course there's only one room. Nothing has gone right. Why should this? She's never slept in the same room with a boy before. Never had to fall asleep to the sound of anyone's breathing but Inez's years ago when they shared a room. And now, here she is, forced to pretend like this is a normal Wednesday for her. Is she supposed to share a bed with this stranger she doesn't even trust? She barely knows anything about him, despite his being her traveling companion across five states and a country border. She grabs her things and follows him to the room at the end of the long building.

"What's your last name?" she asks as he unlocks the door.

"Sharma. Why?"

"No reason."

He turns on the lights, and it's dingier than she expects, seedier. There's an old TV on the left wall, and across from it is a single queen bed. A nightstand sits on either side of it. Paint that had been white at one point has yellowed over the years, giving the room a sickly, inescapable feeling.

"You take the bed. I'll sleep on the floor."

She doesn't argue, though the stained brown carpet does make her pity him for a moment. Instead, she takes Inez's change of clothes and disappears into the bathroom, grateful for the moment alone. She turns on the shower, and cold water sputters out before turning into a sad but steady stream. It'll have to do. She strips and steps beneath it. It is too much to ask it to wash away two days' worth of exhaustion and secrets, but by the time she shuts off the water, she's at least clean. She'll take the small win. Mae stares at her reflection under the harsh fluorescent lighting. Aside from Inez's borrowed lipstick, she hadn't worn or brought any makeup, hadn't planned on having such young and attractive albeit cryptic company. Though she's relieved to know that the thought of him brings forth suspicion more than it does attraction. Small wins.

Her brown eyes look darker than usual in the overhead light, and her short wavy brown hair looks greasy from the stale air of the car and the neon-yellow motel shampoo. The bangs don't seem to sit right, and she regrets cutting them on a whim at three in the morning a week prior. She looks tired. She *is* tired. Multiple stops and two days away from New York and they have just as many answers as they did yesterday—which is to say, next to none. She wishes she'd had more time to ask Ava questions, more time to think of questions to ask. Or at least to know what Ava meant when she said they had a friend in common. Clearly Dev knows him, but does Inez? Is she mixed up in something Mae can only guess at? It still feels impossible to think of Inez dropping fifteen grand as the anonymous buyer after Anthony Mason, but there's something Mae is missing, she can feel it. Can sense that she is on the right track even if she has no idea where it goes.

She quickly changes into whatever she'd blindly grabbed of Inez's clothes. An oversize Florence and the Machine tour T-shirt and a pair of very short shorts that disappear beneath the T-shirt. She thinks of Dev on the other side of the door. Maybe she should have taken an extra second to look through the suitcase. Well, there's nothing to do about it now. They are comfy and this room is warm, too warm. Besides, it is July and a heat wave is rolling through the East Coast—she isn't about to suffer just because of some boy.

She gathers her things and leaves the bathroom to find a shirtless Dev lying on the floor. There isn't much room at the foot of the bed, and so he's taken a pillow and made a makeshift bed to the left of hers. He is sitting with his back to her and doesn't notice as she studies his bare shoulders, the taut muscles down his back. One of the blankets drapes over his lower half, but his bare leg sticks out and she assumes he's wearing boxers underneath there. She blushes at the thought.

He looks up at her as she walks out, and smiles.

"I went to that concert with her. They're even better live, if you can believe it."

Again, this reminder that he is someone of significance in Inez's life. And yet, Mae hadn't heard of him before. She remembers when Inez went to that concert. Mae had made her promise that if they played "My Boy Builds Coffins," she would send a video. And of course, Inez came through. Mae had watched the video on a loop that night, and now, at his words, she has the urge to watch it one more time. Perhaps she missed something.

She sinks into the bed, pulls out her phone, and searches for *Florence* in the chat with her sister. The video quickly comes up, and she grabs her headphones from her bag.

Florence Welch stands in the middle of the stage, ethereal as ever, as the lights dance around her. The edge of the screen is lined with the back of people's heads, an audience just as enthralled as Mae was when she first saw it. She fast-forwards, and there he is looking back at Inez. The lights are bright in that moment, shining on the audience for a split second before moving back to the stage, but there is no denying it is Dev with her sister. Mae rewinds and pauses the video on his face. He smiles right before he turns back to look at Florence. When she checks the messages from that day, she cannot understand why Inez would lie and say she was going alone. Why she wouldn't mention him to Mae, even in passing.

She puts her phone down to find Dev looking at her.

"Good night," he tells her.

"Good night?"

"Yeah?"

"That's it? You're going to sleep? You still haven't explained what happened at Ava's place or why you won't just admit that guy was your brother. We have nowhere to go from here. No plan for tomorrow. And you want to go to sleep?"

"I'm asking you to trust me. Please. Tomorrow, we figure out what to do, together. But right now we're tired, and things will feel clearer in the morning." He looks tired as he says it, like the past days' events have drained him and he is giving her what little there is left of him. *What about her?* she thinks. What about what little there is left of her because he's taken the rest?

She lies back down, frustrated and at a loss for words. He turns off the lamp on the bedside table and she looks at the water-stained ceiling, tinged in green from the neon sign outside. This place is falling apart around her, and all she can do is lie here and let it.

In the silence, "I'm sorry I've been"—he pauses here, searching for the right word—"elusive."

"If you're waiting for me to forgive you, don't hold your breath," she says into the dark.

"I'm not. I just want you to know I'm sorry. That I want to tell you. Even if I can't."

"Why?"

"Why can't I tell you?"

"No, I doubt you'd answer that question. Why do you want to tell me?"

He's quiet for what feels like a minute.

"Because you deserve more than I can give you."

She doesn't know what to make of that, and so she lets the words float between them until they fade into the dark.

The minutes go by. Then the hours. Mae is restless tonight as she waits for Dev to fall asleep. She needs to do something. Anything. And if he won't give her answers, she'll find her own. Eventually, his breathing slows, becomes rhythmic, and she knows he's finally out. She hears his slow breathing, imagines the rise and fall of his broad chest, a few feet away if only she turns on her side. She resists, for a moment, but then she leans over to look at his sleeping face. He's lit by the green neon light peeking through the parted curtains. He's much less annoying now, softer. His full lips are slightly parted and he sleeps on his stomach, his hands tucked beneath his pillow.

There are things he is hiding from her. Secrets he has decided are his alone. But as hard as she racks her brain trying to connect the few dots she has, she knows it is futile. She will only ever guess at the answers he has. She simultaneously wishes she had done this trip alone and yet is relieved Dev, even with all his secrets, is sleeping a few feet from her, as deep in this as she is. Secrets at least allude to answers, even when they are out of her grasp.

Finally, she grabs her backpack with her keys and phone and makes use of her time, two in the morning or not. Outside, the air is even more stifling, a wall she has to push against. She heads to the parking lot, pulls out her keys from her bag, and opens the back of the car. She rummages through the boxes looking for Inez's notebook and research and, once she's found it, slams the back door shut and makes herself comfortable in the driver's seat. Her backpack goes near her feet, and the annotated articles are spread out on the passenger seat. She turns on the overhead light and begins with the notebook, attempting to make out her sister's feverish scrawl. The windows are open, but it makes no difference to the simmering heat rolling in.

Inez's small notebook is a masterpiece, if one enjoys abstract art. The first page, dated four years prior, is legible, for the most part, and begins with a rough history of the white painting as a concept. Some of the information Mae recalls from Henry, the gallery owner, but the rest dives deeper than Henry did. Inez's notes delve into Delphine Lefroy's life, becoming less and less concrete around the time she created the white painting. She speculates when exactly she began it, mentions the same story Henry Hallward told them, about her running away with another woman, but it's clear that Inez doubts that too. There are moments in time where Inez has been able to locate it after Delphine. To a private owner in 1898. On loan to the Metropolitan Museum in 1918. A donation to a New Orleans gallery in 1965.

But then the dates stop, and the question marks come in. Guesses on whether sighted paintings were the same one in question. Theories on where it's traveled and to whom. Accounts of a woman draped in darkness that might connect them. Strange, desperate questions in hopes of finding where it was.

As she flips through, a Polaroid slips out. She turns it over and feels the immediate ache in her chest at the sight of her smiling sister, curls wild and taking up most of the frame. Next to her, a boy leans in to kiss her check. She can't make out much of him, but his buzzed head, the profile of his nose, it's too familiar, too much of a coincidence. The memory of the boy on Ava's doorstep, Dev's brother, is still sharp. Undeniable. Here was proof that they had known each other.

If Inez kept this, and here of all places, then it had to be important to her. *He* had to be important to her. Mae can't understand it. Why keep this from her? What was Inez hiding that she couldn't share with Mae? She thinks back to the book on Inez's coffee table, the first edition of *The Picture of Dorian Gray*, and wonders if it's all connected, if that three-sentence love letter was from the same boy as the one in the picture.

She tucks it back in and focuses on the writing. The notebook shifts from research to journal entries. Pages and pages of notes and thoughts that turn more and more illegible, like she is frantic to find the painting. And she does find it—but where? How? Out of the corner of her eye, a shadow shifts. Mae looks up at the rearview mirror and, for a single fleeting moment, sees a face. Her heart thuds in her chest even after her eyes register the shapes against the canvas, the way the light plays on its harsh surface. She looks over her shoulder and the shifting shadows seem to settle. But now, she can almost swear the paint beneath the peeling corner has an orange glow to it that wasn't there before. The outward curl seems more pronounced, perhaps from the heat, she thinks. Her fingers reach out to touch it, almost involuntarily, and she finds the bent corner is soft against her fingertips, more pliable than she imagined old, dried paint to be. She looks back at the notes and feels the strange sensation of someone reading over her shoulder. She shakes it off. She is alone, after all.

Mae skims through the notes, reading what she can make out, looking for the part where Inez finds the painting, searching for any sort of hint about what came after that can explain where Inez is now. Some faraway part of Mae reminds her that this too is a shot in the dark. That there is no guarantee the painting is even connected to her missing sister. But she shoves the thought aside. Without this, she has nothing. These past two days would have meant nothing. No. She'll reach the end of its line before she sets it aside.

A few pages before the end, she finds it, a name underlined, and the blood rushes from her face. She is as white as the canvas. But only for a second. Just as quickly, she is so full of rage she will combust.

Mae takes the notebook and heads inside. The car door is left ajar in her wake, the overhead light still on, the car running, and she does not care. Mae is a girl on a mission, and the only thing she knows is Dev and the rage that blinds her. She shoves open the door, and the sound of it slamming against the wall jolts Dev awake. He shoots up, bleary-eyed and alert, ready for anything. Though Mae on the attack isn't exactly what he's prepared for.

"What the hell is this?" she says, throwing the notebook at him. The corner of it hits his bare shoulder and he flinches.

"What?" he mumbles as he rubs his eyes. She turns on the lamp between them and he winces at the bulb shining into his eyes. After a second, he picks up the notebook.

He flips through it, looking for answers, but she doesn't have time for him to lie to her. To continue to lie to her. She bends down and rips it from his hands, turns to the page in question, and slams it against his bare chest.

"*The painting was Dev's and now, finally, it's mine.* You lied to me. This whole time you made me think you gave a shit about Inez, that you had no idea what this painting was or why we were on this damn scavenger hunt. But you knew, didn't you?"

"Mae." But he doesn't go on. He stares at the page for what feels like forever. He doesn't make excuses, doesn't try to evade or talk his way out of it. He doesn't do anything at all.

She sits on the floor across from him. Now, finally, sleep is coming. Absolutely and entirely drained, all she wants is to rest her eyes. She's tired of running around looking for answers that don't want to be found, tired of being fooled by the one person she thought she could trust on this strange quest. And especially tired of so easily falling for it. She is tired.

A small thought comes, barely a whisper, and she follows it. "What's beneath the painting? There's something more to it you aren't telling me, isn't there?" she says, asking the question she's put aside since she first reached for the curling corner, since he first stopped her.

"You wouldn't believe me if I told you."

"Fine. I'll find out for myself." She stands and heads to the door.

He jumps up and runs after her. "No!" he yells out.

She isn't surprised when he stops her. He grabs her hand and pulls her toward him. She takes a step back and finds herself pressed against the wall. He is inches away and there is a fierce desperation in his eyes.

"Please. Mae. There are things I can't tell you. This is one of them. Can't that be enough?"

The neon light from the motel sign shines down the open doorway, casting half of him in an emerald hue. The sharp shadows of his shoulders and torso are distinct, and he looks menacing and broken all at once.

In the quite standstill with only an inch between them, a voice booms. "Dev."

With Mae's back to the wall, the open door to her right, she can't see who it is. But a part of her already knows. Dev's expression, a mixture of fear and anger, confirms it.

"Stay here," he says as he moves toward the door.

But Mae isn't one to listen to orders. Especially from people who refuse to explain themselves.

He turns back to find her walking toward him and sighs. No use fighting it. He should have known that.

"I know you're here. I see the car. Will you keep running or finally face me?" the other boy bellows. He is coming from the other side of the parking lot, his white T-shirt bright against the night. He scans the length of the motel until, finally, his eyes land on them.

Mae watches as Dev's jaw tenses.

"Ravi, no. Not here. Not now."

"Then when? Should I come back in another decade when it's a better time for you?"

Another decade? Mae thinks to herself. Dev isn't even twenty.

Dev doesn't say anything. He stands his ground, his fists clenched at his sides. Ravi is mere feet away now, so close she can see the small tear at his collar, the scar on his temple.

"I shouldn't have involved Inez. I won't make that same mistake again," the boy spits out.

"Wait. What do you mean? Do you know where she is?" Mae asks, stepping forward. Suddenly a wave of hurt washes over the man's face. There is love in the bent of his brow, in the way he averts his eyes. Or maybe it's just pain. Mae isn't sure, but she doubts one contradicts the other. He looks back at her, deliberating. There is a quick glance shared between the two brothers until Ravi makes a decision for them. He opens his mouth, but before he can answer, Dev steps forward, winds his fist back, and lands a blow against Ravi's jaw.

Ravi staggers back, but it isn't enough to knock him down. He lunges toward Dev, and Dev stumbles, his injured leg buckling beneath him. Within seconds they are on the ground. Dev twists and pins Ravi down, landing two punches on Ravi's jaw, his shoulder, before Ravi frees his arm and elbows Dev in the nose. Dev's hands go to the blood gushing from his face, and Ravi rolls them both over and punches Dev in the face again. This time, he doesn't stop. Fist to face. Fist to face. Again and again until Dev's arms are no longer blocking his blows. Until he's no longer moving. Dev, in nothing but his boxers, is a quiet heap on the ground, broken and bleeding. Then Ravi finally stops. He stands slowly and looks down at his unconscious brother.

All of this happens in a matter of seconds, and Mae finds herself frozen in place, suddenly feeling very scared to be alone with this man who is willing to beat his own brother to a pulp, much less a stranger. They stare at each other until Mae remembers the car. In her anger, she'd left it running. Even the car door is still open, the overhead light shining down on the painting. She can't help the quick glance she gives it, knows it is a mistake. Ravi follows her eyes, and in that moment, Mae must decide. Does she head for the car and risk fighting, and losing, Ravi for it? She considers her odds, but it is too late. Her moment's hesitation is enough, and the boy runs. In a matter of seconds, he dives into the car and drives away, the tires skidding against the gravel as he floors it out of the motel parking lot. He takes everything they have with him. The car, the painting, her backpack, all her sister's things, disappear past the tree line.

Chapter 10

Dev walks home in a daze. He feels as if he has been woken from a dream not yet whole. He wants to shake it off, to forget the entire exchange. But the name Delphine Lefroy echoes in his head, impossible to ignore. He can feel every reverberation like a thud against his skull.

Delphine Lefroy.

Delphine Lefroy.

Delphine Lefroy.

No. He knows he won't forget this, and besides, he does not want to. The woman has given him something in the shape of a gift, and he cannot bear to leave it wrapped.

He approaches the wrought iron gates that separate his home from the outside world and opens them with a key. They creak against the weight of his arm.

In front of him is Rowan Manor. Its four floors and wide-set windows feel garish in the mornings, but here, now that the moonlight has softened its edges, he can almost admire its arching roofs, the thick round turret that juts out just off the center. But this is not his home. He walks toward the manor and then right past it to the cottage near the back where his family has lived all his life.

"Dev, is that you?"

He turns around, disoriented for a second before he finds the boy the voice belongs to. Nik.

The boy smiles. He stands in the greenhouse, beautifully framed by the glass doorway. His edges are lit by a nearby lantern, and for a single moment, Dev forgets the unrelenting echo in his head.

"You're out late," Dev says. And the boy steps forward with a sketchbook in his hand, which he holds out toward him eagerly.

"There's evening primrose growing in the greenhouse, see?" he says, pointing to the page. His straight auburn hair falls toward his dark green eyes and he moves it away with a quick hand.

Nik has drawn an intricate portrait of the flower, its leaves thick and heavy, the petals round and sharp at the point. Beneath it, he's written *Oenothera biennis* in soft, delicate script.

"They only bloom at night."

Dev looks up from the paper to see Nik staring at him, and he wonders if he's waiting for his approval or something more. Either way, he feels his face warm under Nik's gaze and looks away to calm his flushed cheeks.

"Have you seen Ravi?" Dev says quickly, clearing his throat.

Nik shakes his head, shutting his sketchbook and gently sliding it into his satchel. "I don't think he's come out all day. Most likely holed up somewhere reading." He stretches, pulling the edge of his white button-up loose from his trousers. Dev can't help but watch as a sliver of skin appears, then disappears. He turns his eyes away.

Dev knows he should have been home too, should have stayed put, and then maybe he wouldn't be wondering about a woman named Delphine Lefroy. A not-so-secret part of him is thrilled at the thought of setting off on this strange adventure by himself. Another part of him feels overwhelmed at the idea of setting off alone, *being* alone. It is a strange thing to be. He does not think he has ever done it. His hands have always been in search of company, his mind reaching to fill space before the quiet sets in. If there is a way to avoid his thoughts, he will find it.

"Are you all right?" Nik asks, bringing him back. Dev looks back at him for a second, contemplating. He wonders what Nik and Ravi would think if he told them of the woman in the shadows, of what she'd told him. Would they laugh, think him mad? Would they come along? But their answers are irrelevant because Dev can't set off to God knows where in search of Delphine Lefroy and nothing else. It is unthinkable. No, he will set it aside.

He nods. "Just tired, I should head home." The boys say their goodbyes and part ways, Nik to the manor and Dev to the cottage. By the time he wakes the next morning, he will have forgotten the entire exchange, he's sure of it.

He is wrong.

After a fitful sleep, Dev wakes with the same two words on his tongue. He shoves them aside, going about his day like any other. A trip to town with Ravi, classes at the nearby college, a drink with a friend. He comes home to find his father, and though he should feel relieved that he isn't in a volatile mood, Dev can't bring himself to feel anything. All day, he has had the strange sensation of watching over himself, of being separate. Elsewhere.

That night, he dreams of the woman made of shadows, dreams of her bathed in darkness, and when he wakes, he checks the corners of his room, beneath his bed, unsure if it was a dream or if she is as real as he is. He spends the day in a daze, going from one task to another. A walk in the woods with Nik, a quiet meal as he feeds his ailing mother. She looks at him, unblinking, and he averts his eyes, certain that, though he hasn't uttered a word about this to anyone, she can see right through to his deepest thought.

When night comes, he dreads having to sleep. Again, the woman made of shadows visits his dreams. She walks toward him, a beacon in the black abyss. He does not know what to call her, he realizes. She never gave him a name. And yet, with certainty he cannot explain, he knows there isn't one.

The woman trails a finger against his jaw and, without opening her mouth, whispers *Delphine Lefroy*. Dev wakes with a start, his chest heaving as if he'd been running. To his left, he finds Ravi still asleep, the early morning sunlight landing on his sheets in wide arcs.

Why him? he wonders as he falls back into his pillow. Why did she have to find him? What he would do to think of anything else, but he is finally coming to terms with the fact that there is no forgetting this. The question now is what he will do with it.

He spends the day looking for an opportunity to tell Ravi and Nik. But no moment feels right. He does not know how to phrase it. How to convince them of what he's seen. He wouldn't fault them for thinking him mad. He wonders it himself.

As the day comes to a close, Dev steps outside into the crisp fall air and wonders if he will spend another fitful night avoiding what he now knows is inevitable.

In the greenhouse is Nik drawing by moonlight; the plants surround him, and he looks as if he's blooming within them. Dev doesn't give himself a chance to hesitate. He walks toward Nik, but before he realizes it, he's running.

Nik looks at him with curious eyes as Dev runs into the greenhouse and comes to a stop in front of him. He pauses to catch his breath.

"I have to tell you something," Dev says, and the other boy's brow furrows.

"Sounds incredibly serious."

"It is. Possibly. I don't know yet. But I want to find out. With you."

Nik smiles. "I'm listening."

"Let's find Ravi." And he grabs hold of Nik's hand. The two boys run off toward the cottage.

An Interlude

1964

*I*n the warm glow of the fireplace sit two women. The silence is especially loud tonight as they wait. They listen to the soft crackle of the fire, watch as the flames lick the wood. They glance at each other with curious eyes, asking the same question: Why are we here? Finally, Mary, their hostess and friend, returns with a tray of three teacups filled to the brim. A bowl of sugar and a small spoon rest in the middle. She sets the tray down on the coffee table and stares at them both.

"Won't you sit?" the first woman, Katherine, asks.

Mary shakes her head and smiles. "I'm much too excited to sit still."

When they both look at her, as if waiting for her to speak, she only motions toward the tea.

"Mary, no," the woman on the other couch, Norma, says. "We've been patient, but you're acting strange. Why are we here?"

"Can't a woman have a night with her closest friends?" Mary says.

"Sure, but this isn't that, is it? Something's happened."

"You sounded frantic on the phone. Urgent," Katherine adds.

Mary is quiet for a moment as her friends stare at her, waiting.

She looks at the mantel. Above the fireplace hangs a white painting in an ornate golden frame. The top right corner of the paint curls outward.

"Recently, Owen and I came across this painting, gifted to us by a friend of his father's."

It appears bare, but the two women squint in the dim room, trying to make out a shape, an outline, anything. Shadows appear to twist and contort against the canvas, but they are only those of the flickering flames that fill the room.

"What is it?" Katherine asks. She tilts her head, as if the blank canvas will answer.

Mary smiles. "Ladies, there is quite the history behind this painting. But what's even more interesting are the rumors."

And within the glow of the fire, Mary tells them a story of want and magic and love. And though it is all based on tales passed down in whispers, it is, surprisingly, mostly true.

Hours later, the cups of untouched tea have gone cold.

The three women are long gone.

Only the painting remains.

Chapter 11

Dev is on the ground. Beneath the blood gushing from his nose, his lip is cut and a bruise blossoms on his cheek. There's another cut at the edge of his eyebrow, and Mae wipes the wet red streaming down near his eye.

"Dev," Mae says, shaking him. Her hand goes to his throat and she searches for a pulse. She feels it, a faint rhythm beneath his warm skin, and sighs in relief.

Slowly, he stirs, and Mae helps him stand. He groans as he gets to his feet and then winces as he holds his side. He is bent at the waist for a second before taking a deep breath and squaring his shoulders.

"You okay?" she asks, though it's clear he's far from it. He nods and looks around, his eyes scanning the parking lot until they stop on the empty parking space where her car was a few minutes ago.

"He took it?"

"He took everything. The painting. Inez's things. My backpack. Even my phone. I shouldn't have left the keys in the car. It's my fault." She runs her fingers through her hair in frustration, balling up strands in her fists before letting go. She has lost so much, but for some reason, her mind goes to the broken charcoal in the backpack pocket she hasn't touched in weeks, to a month-old granola bar from when she was still in school.

He shakes his head, but even that small act seems to hurt. He closes his eyes for a moment, collecting his breath, and looks at her.

"You couldn't have known. He must have checked the motels in the area, looking for us. I should have kept driving, created more distance between us and him."

"You couldn't have known," Mae says, and he smiles. The cut on his lip bleeds, and he gently wipes it away with his thumb.

She sighs. "Let's get you cleaned up."

He follows her back inside to the bathroom and she turns on the fluorescent lighting. It flickers for a moment before settling. Beneath the harsh light, the bruises on his skin are quickly worsening.

"Sit."

He listens and slowly lowers his body to the edge of the bathtub, letting her take charge. Mae can see he is tired in more ways than one. Seeing Ravi has taken something from him. She takes note of the open cut near his eyebrow, the blood around his potentially broken nose. His split lip. She doesn't let her eyes linger on his torso, on the hint of abs against tender bruises. Instead, she takes a towel and soaks it under the warm tap.

Dev closes his eyes as she softly presses the damp towel to his skin. She wipes a splatter of blood on his neck, but with one hand at the back of his head and the other wiping the red from his throat, this part of his body feels more charged than the rest. She moves on, and he winces when she pats the open cut on his forehead. Her hand goes back to the nape of his neck to hold him in place.

"Don't move."

"Sorry." He looks at her as he says it, and instantly, she can feel her pulse quicken. There is a moment that stretches for minutes, hours, days as she presses the cloth against his skin until she finally looks away to resoak the towel. In the close proximity of the bathroom, there is nowhere for her to go to not feel him. She feels his gaze on her at the sink, brushes against his knee when she turns. He is everywhere, and she finds that she must remind herself of her anger, of lies and betrayal and all those other words she felt not too long ago. But he is looking at her with such focus, such intensity, that her memory dissipates like smoke.

"Thank you," he says. He squeezes her hand. A quick second before it's over, before she has time to react. She looks down and it's back to gripping the edge of the bathtub almost as if she imagined it.

"You should really consider a boxing class or something. That was painful to watch."

"Yeah, probably. I was never the athlete of the two of us." He smiles, but it only makes him look sadder. She rummages around the dingy cabinet and finds an old first aid kit from at least twenty years ago. Still, there's a small Band-Aid and so she rips it open. She looks at the cut, the shape of it deep and wide, and is unsure how best to stop the bleeding. The last time she dealt with blood that wasn't her period was a scraped knee from a bike ride gone wrong in the tenth grade. She also doesn't feel qualified to stamp a Band-Aid on a wound still oozing down his temple.

"Here," he says when he sees her hesitation. He leans forward to catch a glimpse of himself in the mirror. Using the small pair of scissors inside the kit, he cuts the long Band-Aid into two thin, sticky strips and, with deft fingers, squeezes the cut closer together. He applies both strips perpendicular to the wound and leans back to his original position.

He sees her bewilderment and laughs. "I have experience in wound care."

"That's not vague at all," she says before shaking her head. "Why would you punch him if you knew you couldn't beat him?" She wipes the blood from around his mouth and he waits until she's done before responding.

"I do a lot of things I can't justify. Rational, logical. They're not the first words people would use to describe me." She looks at him for a second as he says it, and he gives her a small shrug.

Stepping back to look at her work, she only now sees the darker part of his jeans, the way it seems plastered onto his leg. He winces when she touches it, her hand coming back red.

"It's fine. I'm okay." He gently rolls up the fabric, and a gash, wide and deep, reveals itself. Mae can't comprehend how Ravi would have been able to do that during the fight, but Dev doesn't seem surprised to see it. He tightly wraps his leg in gauze, the blood already seeping through the material before he's even pulled his pant leg back down.

He isn't concerned, and so Mae decides not to question it. In the strangeness of this night, this seems inconsequential. "Okay, you're done." It's not impossible his nose is broken, but there's nothing she can do about it.

"Thanks," he says again as he stands. The space between them is nonexistent as she remembers only in this moment how tall he is. Their eyes meet, and she holds his gaze for longer than necessary. When her eyes fall to his lips, she thinks he'll lean forward that final inch. Mae doesn't know if she wants him to, and yet, she doesn't move, doesn't look away. But after a few seconds he steps away and clears his throat.

"Are you hungry?" he asks. Before she can answer, he decides for them. "There's a diner down the road."

She shakes off the surprising wave of disappointment, the bitter taste of near rejection, and nods. Tired or not, Mae knows the likelihood of her actually sleeping tonight is low, and so there is no use fighting it. It's always a good time for breakfast.

They begin to gather their things, which at this point aren't much. Dev buttons up the shirt he's been wearing for the past two days and grabs his wallet. His fingers move gingerly over the fabric, careful not to touch his bruised torso. Mae realizes that she had stuffed her overalls and crop top into her back-pack, which is now miles away with Ravi. She tries not to think of her pencils and sketchbook, also long gone.

She finds Inez's notebook on the ground and picks it up. The Polaroid has slipped out, and so she tucks it back into the pages. She's anxious over her missing phone, dreads having to figure out how to tell her parents the car was stolen, or how to even get home to tell them, but Inez's notebook fills her with relief. This notebook holds answers to questions Mae doesn't even know to ask yet. She just needs time. Time to decipher Inez's hurried writing, time to understand what she was doing those final days. Time for Dev to open up. They shut the door behind them and make their way to the diner. On Dev is his wallet, Henry Hallward's business card, and his phone. Mae carries nothing but Inez's notebook.

Dev is leaning on his cane more than usual to dull the pain in his side, the open wound on his knee. There's no sidewalk here, and so they tread along the grass as cars rush past them on their way to wherever it is they need to go at three in the morning.

Mae's thoughts wander to the woman in the white house. To her cheating husband and if he really left her or if his disappearance is connected to Inez's. There is a bias to her approach, to the way she searches for any scrap of sinister intent, any clue to lead them to a plan. To anything instead of slowly walking toward a diner as Ravi gets farther and farther away. She remembers the note in Henry Hallward's file, *Call Ravi*, and her heart lurches as she realizes it must have been their Ravi. He must have known they'd go to the last owner's house, must have called Ava and had her promise she'd let him know if they came, must have been lying in wait.

How did Ravi know someone would come looking?

And—her breath catches in triumph—that must mean

there's something to be found. Suddenly, it doesn't feel like she's grasping for clues, only uncovering them.

Dev doesn't say anything as they walk toward the diner, their arms occasionally bumping against each other. But she hopes food, AC, time, will loosen the tight grip he has on the answers she needs.

They sit down and the chatter of the diners quiets. Sure, Mae is a disheveled mess in her shorts and T-shirt so long that it looks like she forgot to wear pants. And Dev is bruised and bleeding, limping more than usual as they walk to an empty table. But they're also two brown kids in the middle of a clearly white town. She wonders which part caught the room's attention first.

A few minutes later, a waitress takes their order: coffee, pancakes, orange juice. The wooden table is sticky beneath their hands, and the hanging light above their booth seems to be swaying of its own accord. Dev reaches to steady it and then goes back to tugging at his worn leather bracelet. He doesn't look at her once, too focused on his wrist, the marks on the table, the late-night customers as they resume their chatter. By the time the food comes, Mae feels like she has given him all the time she is capable of giving. But before she can ask him all the questions that want to come spilling from her mouth, he begins.

"In 1891, I was eighteen years old."

"Excuse me?" she says with a laugh. She isn't sure what she was expecting, but it was never this.

He shakes his head, starts again. "In 1891, I was eighteen years old for the first time. I met a woman made of shadows, and she led me to a painting made of want. A painting with the power to give me everything I could have desired."

"You're serious," she says, and her smile has slipped away. In its place is curiosity tinged with fear. She does not want to believe him. Does not know how to. But it is clear he means every word he says.

"For so long, all I wanted was to leave. My family was—" He pauses here, frowning, searching. His features, a shadow of anger and something else Mae can't place. "Isolating. Complicated. Ravi is my twin. But he didn't have that same need for escape. He wanted other things for himself, dangerous, selfish things, but never that. One night, a woman approached me in the woods. I didn't know what she was, not for sure, anyway, but she was something beyond us, and only the devil could offer what she was offering. I still remember how she smiled at me like . . . like she knew every thought I'd ever tried to keep in the dark." Dev seems lost in thought before his eyes snap back to her. "She came to me with a proposal: Find Delphine Lefroy and her painting, and in return, I would get what I most wanted in this world. I should have known it wouldn't be that simple. But Ravi and I set out to find it all the same, hoping that whatever magic lived at the end of our journey, it would be enough for the both of us to share."

He studies her face to see if he has said too much. They're both quiet for a beat before Mae asks, "What did Ravi want?"

Dev sighs and leans forward. "Ravi had a fear of dying. Not necessarily of death itself. Death was a moment, imminent. Out of our hands. Death would come, and beyond its door, no one knew. Dying, though, was different. Dying was decay. It was your body betraying you. It was your cells dying faster than they can regenerate, and in some cases, it was your *mind* dying a quicker death than the rest of you. There is no greater fear for Ravi than this."

A booth over, a woman laughs, and it cuts their moment in half, a reminder that they aren't alone.

"I did not have these fears," he continues in a whisper, staring at his coffee instead of Mae. "I had come to accept life could be unfair, and so there was no use fearing what would come. We had seen it after all, in the way our mother had been bedridden since we were twelve years old by ALS, though we didn't know it then. We'd seen it in our father's bruised fists and sharp tongue. Life could be cruel, but we had each other, and for me, that was enough."

"But not for Ravi?" she asks, though it sounds more like a statement.

He shakes his head. "Ravi wanted more, needed more. He had seen those same things and wanted desperately for something greater than simply running away. And so when the opportunity arose to take matters into his own hands, who could blame him for trying. No matter the cost. I've always wondered whether he had given away our souls, whether, if death ever came for us, we'd have to give those up too. He agreed so quickly, he hadn't even thought to ask. In the end, the deal was this: In an effort to escape death and dying altogether, youth, everlasting life, would forever be tied to this painting. The same way we two brothers would always be tied to each other. One's fate, the other's tragedy, one gifted with eternal life, the other cursed to live forever. There is no separating one side of the coin from the other."

"But why force you into this?" Mae asks. "This was Ravi's wish. Not yours."

He stirs his coffee but doesn't drink it. After a moment, he answers. "We entered this world together, as twins, bound by blood. She thought it would be fitting that we'd be bound by this too. Though I've never believed that to be the reason. I think she just wanted to see how far he was willing to go, if he would do it. And he did. Ravi struck a deal with a sort of devil knowing it would apply to me as well. I had no need for eternal youth. Had no want to avoid what came beyond that door. I lived and, eventually, hoped to die. Only one of us would get what we wanted."

He takes a deep breath and leans back, like giving her his life story has taken something from him. She isn't sure what questions to ask first. The ones that had been brewing in her mind when she sat down are long gone.

"You're immortal." She says it out loud, testing out the words on her tongue.

"Sort of. I think immortal in the way you know it wouldn't be all that accurate."

"But if I stabbed you right now, you wouldn't die," she says, picking up the butter knife.

"Actually, I could. Maybe not with that," he says, nodding toward the dull knife in her hand. "But I'm mortal in that my body is as fragile as yours. It's just that—I don't—" He stops himself here, unsure of how to continue. "It's complicated."

"Try," she says firmly. She's not moving until she gets her answers. She will undo him, she decides. Will pull back every layer until there are no secrets left to hide. Inez is enough mystery for them both. Dev doesn't need to be one too.

"We age, yes," he tries again. "But as long as we sacrifice people to the painting, our bodies reset to the moment the deal was made. It's dying we've escaped. Not death. I live and I live and I live. And if Ravi keeps sacrificing innocent people to the painting, that's all I'll ever do."

"What do you mean 'sacrifice people'?" Mae's heart races to connect the dots before he answers.

"The painting needs to be fed. Ravi targets victims, and over time, as the edge curls, curiosity gets the best of them, and they pull it back. It—it takes them. And with every life, time resets for us. Eighteen once again, the bodies we had the night the deal was made. But as time wore on, so did the painting. As the wooden frame softened and the gold foil frayed, and as the canvas withered, so did the painting's power. It took longer for our bodies to reset back to eighteen. Months instead of minutes. Faster for us to age forward. Years instead of decades. Which meant the painting needed more lives than before and it needed them faster to give back what we, what Ravi, had been promised."

"That's why you didn't want me to pull at the peeling edge." Her eyes go wide as the pieces click into place.

He nods. "I couldn't let you be another sacrifice. I had spent so long failing to save a single soul from his grasp. And though all I wanted was to die, I couldn't sit there and let Ravi continue to sacrifice people just to prolong his own overdue death." He says all of this matter-of-factly, but there is a somberness beneath his surface. She can see it seeping out.

Mae has so many questions. But only one matters. "And Inez?" It comes out as a whisper. "How does she come into all of this?"

He pauses, deliberating on where to begin, where to pick up. She can tell that there is so much between then and now, that he is sifting through lifetimes to find what she needs to know. "Sometimes we lost sight of the painting. It has a way of making itself scarce, winding up in museum collections, in musty basements and dank ships. I don't know if I'm looking for patterns. You can find anything if you look long enough, and one hundred thirty-three years is plenty long," he tells Mae. "We always get it back. Or more accurately, Ravi always gets it back. Always one step ahead of me.

"Until last year, when I was able to steal it back. After over a hundred years of the chase, of trying to take it from him and destroy it, of trying to put an end to this more-than-a-century-long sentence, I had finally won. But alone with the painting for the first time, I froze. I panicked. Destroying it would be permanent. I would kill us both. I knew I should. I knew in time I would, but I wasn't ready. When it came down to it, I wanted one final taste of life. And then I would do it. I would end it all for both of us. I thought I was safe. Ravi didn't know where I lived. In all likelihood, he didn't know I had the painting. I was the one who bought it in cash from Henry Hallward last year. I think he recognized me, he just couldn't place me."

Mae recalls the brief moment when Henry saw Dev, the confusion in his eyes that was quickly overtaken by the curiosity for the painting, the urge to tell them all about it.

"Anyway, after months of stalling, in December I packed a bag, locked up my apartment, and went off on a final adventure with the plan that once I returned, I'd end it all. For the both of us. By the time I'd come back, it was too late. Inez stole it before I had the chance to finally destroy it. It was my fault for not taking the chance when I had it."

He sees her hesitation, her want to trust him. He does not push her. Instead, he sits in the silence, letting Mae take the lead. She wonders about what he isn't saying, about the spaces between the lines. That maybe fear fueled his resentment, that as much as dying scared Ravi, death scared Dev. But even if she wants every detail she can pull out of him, there's only one part of this she needs.

"What did Ravi mean when he said he shouldn't have involved Inez, that he won't make that same mistake again?"

"We know Ravi knew Inez, that they must have planned this together, deliberately taken the painting from me so Ravi would get it back." Here, his confidence falters. "But something must have happened between the plan and her going missing. Maybe she changed her mind, refused to tell him where it was. Maybe he took her, hoping she'd finally cave. Maybe he's had her for months, hoping she'd break. I was shocked when we found the painting in her apartment but"—he pauses, looks up at her—"I didn't want to tell you it was mine or you'd think I had something to do with her disappearance."

Mae understands the lie. Still, she thinks of all the time they wasted. If only she had known the truth. "So when we went to the gallery, we gave Ravi the opening, the cracked door he's been looking for," she says, getting them back on track.

"Exactly."

"So how do we know Inez is out there, that she isn't already inside the painting?" The panic in her voice is palpable; she is desperate for him to tell her it's not too late. That Inez hasn't been with them all along.

"If Ravi did it, he would have taken the painting with him immediately. The fact that she's missing and the painting was still in her apartment is proof enough."

She sees the logic in his thinking, but her own cynical train of thought wins. "What if she pulled it back herself?"

"She knew, Mae." He reaches forward and picks up Inez's notebook between them. "Clearly. Look at all the research, the journal, conspiring with Ravi. She knew what she was doing."

"But now. Now, if you're right, if he really has her, then she's in danger. He has both. He could sacrifice her to it now, couldn't he? Clearly, she knows too much."

His grip falters. She sees his urge to placate her, to disregard the worry, but he'd be lying to her and he's done enough of that already. What she deserves is his honesty.

"It's possible," he says, sighing. "They planned this together until they didn't, until she got the painting and decided to keep it for herself, or realized it was too much power for him to have. I don't know. Maybe he wouldn't."

She thinks he'll end there but he reconsiders.

"But he lacked a soul before that devil ever got involved. Ravi has sacrificed people he cared for in the past. Why would this be any different?"

She sees his tense jaw, his averted eyes. There is pain in their history, but she doesn't push. She lets him keep this part of himself. She's too focused on what he's confirmed, anyway. That Inez could be in danger, somewhere out there only Ravi knows.

"I should have put an end to it when I had the chance. This is all my fault," he says, his head in his hands. "If we can just find him, we can get it back, destroy it once and for all."

"By destroy it, you mean . . . kill yourself."

He gives her a weak smile and shrugs. "Don't worry about me. I've lived more than my fair share."

She hesitates. His ask is simple, reasonable, but how can she help him kill himself, kill his brother? Is she capable of that, no matter how long they've both lived? She doesn't know how she can continue this journey knowing there is only one way it can end. But how can she not, knowing her sister could be at the end of it?

"Look," he says, assuaging her hesitance. "I could have done this years ago, could have ended it all for myself right when it began. But Ravi chose this life for the both of us. He knew what I wanted, and he chose this anyway, and—" He hesitates.

"And you haven't found a way to forgive him for that." She finishes for him. He doesn't disagree. "A hundred and thirty-three years is a long time to hold a grudge."

He doesn't answer at first. Only sits there and tries to put the words together, to make her understand what he can barely justify. "I thought in time, I could let it go, could let him have what he wanted and end my half of the deal. Kill myself. Simple enough. But my anger has festered. It consumes too much of me. There is so little left." He even sounds hollow.

"I can understand that."

Mae surprises them both and reaches for his hand beyond the stack of pancakes. She squeezes once and lets go, but only then realizes that she likes holding his hand, that touching him feels warm. Safe.

He looks up with a questioning look. "Does this mean you believe me?"

"Should I not?"

"I can't exactly prove it, can I? Cut me and I'll bleed. Run me over and I'll die."

She looks at him for a moment, considering. "Here's the thing. If you're lying to me, there's no way what actually happened is stranger than this. It would be a lot easier to tell me the truth than to make all this up, and you're choosing this. I'm taking it as fact. Still, I wish you told me sooner," she says, leaning back against the cracked leather of the booth.

"I barely know how to tell you now, let alone two minutes after meeting you. 'Hi, I'm Dev,'" he says, waving. "'I think your sister stole the painting that makes me sort of immortal'?"

"Fine." She resists the urge to smile.

His shoulders relax, relieved he doesn't have to convince her even if there is nowhere for them to go from here. But Mae is tired of feeling helpless. She sits straight up and looks at Dev as he stirs the long-dissolved sugar in his coffee.

"This isn't a dead end."

"How?"

"Because I say it isn't."

He smiles. "Okay. This isn't a dead end. What now?"

"Now we go after Ravi, get the painting back, and find Inez."

"Easy." He huffs, disbelieving.

She thinks for a moment, and then the answer seems so obvious, she isn't sure why neither of them has said it yet.

"He took my car. But he must have gotten here somehow. Maybe there's something in his, something that could tell us where he's going next."

Just like that they have a clue, at least enough of one to get going. So Dev nods and gets up. He throws a twenty on the table, and the two head back to the motel parking lot in search of the only lead they have left.

Last November

Inez sits in Dev's apartment, eyeing the painting that rests on his kitchen wall. She sips her glass of white wine as Dev moves around the island, preparing dinner. He is telling her about the new Van Gogh art exhibit at the Met, but the words slip through her ears. She's too absorbed to listen; her eyes can't pull away from that alabaster canvas, or the way its shadows seem to slope and streak under the soft lighting.

"Inez?" he says, and his voice pulls her out of its spell. She takes a sip of her wine and looks at him.

"Hmm?"

"I said, are you ready for dinner?" He holds two plates of pasta, cacio e pepe made from scratch, and looks at her, waiting. It's not until then that the smell of butter, fresh-cracked pepper, and cheese hits her, and suddenly she's famished. She can't remember the last time she ate. They move to his small dining table and she spins a forkful into her mouth before he's even sat down.

"I'm glad this last dinner worked out. Six months is a long time without my favorite neighbor."

"Six months?"

"South America? I leave next week. You knew that."

"Of course I did." But it must have slipped her mind because now her brain is connecting the dots, finding her way through what has felt like a four-year maze. And here, finally, she can see that wonderous exit. She looks at the painting hanging over his shoulder, and tonight, it seems to look back.

Chapter 12

"You can't be serious." Ravi looks at Dev, incredulous. He sits in a tattered yellow velvet chair in the corner of the room he shares with Dev, a thick book on his lap. His fingers tease at the torn corner of the cover.

"Why would I make this up?"

Dev turns to Nik, hoping, praying, his oldest friend might be quicker to believe him than his brother. Nik sits on Dev's bed, his eyes darting between both brothers before landing on Dev.

"It sounds completely absurd. And of course I believe him," Nik says with steady determination, as if Dev has shared an unshakable truth.

Relief rushes through Dev, and he can feel his shoulders release at Nik's words. He may not have Ravi on board, but Nik is and maybe that's enough.

"Gentlemen, this is preposterous. A woman appears, most likely feral and living in the woods, tells you of a mysterious painting and a name, and you plan to simply trust her? To have us pack up our things and go in search of what exactly? Some fanciful wish to be granted? To live out some fantasy? You don't even know where this Delphine is." He looks at them, sure that he's made them see sense, but then Nik breaks the silence.

"Actually," he says with an awkward smile, as if it hurts him to prove Ravi wrong, "my family knows Lefroys out in Chicago. They might not be the same ones, but it's a start?"

Dev looks at his brother as he points to Nik. "Chicago! What is that? A day's journey away? We'll be back by Friday."

"Oh God, you're serious."

"Yes," Dev says. "I'm going. Nik is too." Dev looks over at him, hoping he hasn't made a wrong assumption, but Nik nods and stands firm, his broad shoulders pulled back and ready, as if they were beginning this adventure right then and there.

"Come with us, Ravi," Nik says, and the two share a look that Dev isn't quite sure how to read. For a moment, he is convinced Nik and Ravi know something he doesn't, that there is an entire conversation happening in front of him in a secret language he's never heard. But the moment passes, and Ravi looks back at Dev with slightly less skepticism.

"We're going to be back in two days with nothing to show for it but wasted train fare."

"And a story to tell," Nik says with a smile.

"I regret this already," Ravi says as he rolls his eyes, and the other two share a grin.

"We'll leave in the morning," Dev says. Already plans are racing through his head—the arrangements they'll have to make for their mother's care, perhaps with a maid they can pay for the two days they'll be gone, the money they'll need, not to mention keeping this from their father. He glances at his brother, and they share a look nearly two decades old, one all too familiar with an unstable father. This they'll discuss once Nik leaves. Once he walks home through the garden, opens the glass back double doors, takes the mahogany staircase up to the second floor, and walks down the too-long corridor to the room he shares with no one and sinks into his silk sheets—for Rowan Manor, of course, is his. Only once all their roles on this estate are reaffirmed will they discuss the private intricacies of this plan, or at least the parts of themselves that have always felt too shameful to share with Nik.

Niklaus Rowan, after all, will inherit all of this. Including the cottage they currently reside in. The three may have grown up together, may know one another just as well as any people could, but he will always be the boy this all belongs to, and they will always be the sons of his gardener.

And so they begin: They will leave at sunrise. Their father, if he has drunkenly made it home by then, will be fast asleep. They will leave a note for him to find once they are miles away.

Their father hasn't always been like this. The boys have fond memories of him when they lived in India as children. Of evenings spent in the grand garden of their lavish home as their parents laughed together. Of secret trips before dinner for syrup-soaked jalebi. Back when their father would conspire with them in Hindi, before he had distanced himself from it altogether in an effort to assimilate to people that wanted nothing to do with him. The brothers find it difficult to speak the language after all these years, tongues stumbling over what had once been their first language. Their mother held on to it for as long as she could, before that too was taken from her. Nowadays, the only times they hear Hindi is on their father's lips, when it is laced in venom.

But it is not impossible to understand what happens to a man when he loses the money and power he has become accustomed to. When he has everything and then moves to America in search of more, only to find he must bend at the whims of far more powerful men.

It's Ravi who reminds Dev what to bring. It's Ravi who finds the train schedules and plans their route—one stop in Pennsylvania to transfer trains halfway through. It's Ravi who makes three sandwiches and carefully wraps them in paper for the trip. This trip that was never his idea, that he had resisted the whole way through. And yet, here he is gingerly spreading a thick layer of cream cheese against a piece of sourdough bread. It is a day old, the edges harder than they should be, but it will do. Ravi does everything with care, even when he vehemently disagrees.

Ravi goes back to their room and sits on the hardwood. Dev, off to make arrangements for their mother's care, will be back soon. He doesn't mind having to do the rest if it means his brother will handle what he can't. He lifts the corner of the thin rug, exposing a loose floorboard. The boys had discovered it years ago, and ever since then, it has been turned into a trove of meaningless treasures. Broken but sentimental toys, special rocks, loose change found on the road like flecks of gold, and at one point, one snail carefully tucked inside by a young Dev.

With nowhere to go, it died soon after, and Ravi had discreetly done away with it before Dev could see.

These days the floorboards are lined with modest piles of cash they have spent years adding to. It isn't significant by any means, but it will be more than enough to get them through the trip. Ravi places them in the bottom of his bag, underneath a change of clothes, the book he's been reading, and three sandwiches he packs carefully on top. He won't admit this to Dev, too fixated on being the realistic brother, but there is a nervous excitement rolling through his body, one that reminds him he has not been farther west than Syracuse all his life. He remembers the thrill of crossing the Vermont border to New York years ago, inconsequential compared with the journey he is about to embark on.

Dev returns and the two share a look before silently agreeing to go talk to their mother. Their father, still not home, is an absence they must be wary of, like walking around the edge of a black hole to avoid falling in. They don't know when he'll be back, but the worry lives in them both. For now, they walk down the hall to their mother's room, where she lies in bed. Her eyes are closed, but when she hears her sons, she opens them.

Ravi and Dev have spent years watching their mother crawl into herself against her will. Years of words turned to silence, of laughter turned to quiet. For six years, the boys watched as their mother lost control of her body one bit at a time. Until she was bedridden, frozen in place. She blinks at the boys, but it is all she can do now. The doctors are no help, they've only abandoned her as she drifts further away from shore, from the woman she once was.

Dev sits to her left as Ravi, a few feet away, leans against the doorframe. Ravi glances around the room, his eyes catching on anything that isn't their slowly dying mother.

Dev doesn't expect him to come any closer. He is ashamed to admit how much he would rather have left this task to Ravi, but that has never been their arrangement. Dev has always borne the brunt of this, has seen its horrors up close, witnessed their mother lose pieces of herself every day. Being around her ailing like this fills him with such a heavy ache in his chest, he's convinced it'll drag him down to the floor and keep him there. In his darkest moments, the same thought creeps in: That he has inherited her illness the way he inherited her brown eyes. Her wide smile and her infectious laugh. A laugh he can barely remember, now. Oh, what he would do to save her from this. Dev clears his throat, leans forward, and begins.

Ravi listens silently as Dev tells her the truth. All of it. The woman Dev met bathed in shadows and the promise she made him. They'll be back in two days' time, they say. They don't know if she believes them, if she thinks these are silly tales from boys too old to tell them, but they find that they do not lie. Her days are too shortly numbered to speak anything but the truth—and though they will not admit it, it comes easy, knowing she can do nothing to stop them. Which makes her one of the few people who know them entirely. She blinks at them, pressing her eyes closed, an acknowledgment of a sort, and Ravi watches as Dev squeezes her hand before kissing her on the forehead. They feel lighter the moment they step out of her room.

Dev sleeps a restless sort of sleep, one that has him waking and stirring, until dawn's arrival is a relief. Adrenaline courses through them both as they gather their things, and though they've barely slept for more than four hours, they feel more alert than ever.

They head downstairs, a prayer on their lips—but it goes unanswered.

There near the front door stands their father. He stumbles forward as both boys appear, bags in hand.

"What is this?" he says, and it is so quiet that the silence echoes in his words' wake. The slight slur puts both boys on edge. Their father sober is dangerous, but drunk he is unpredictable.

"We'll be back," Ravi says. He knows to be sparing with his words. Knows to listen for the sound beneath his father's sentences. Understands that underneath his father's anger is fear. Of being left alone with her. Of being abandoned entirely. Ravi hopes it will be enough, the assurance that they'll be back for him. That though one day they may leave him, this is not that day.

His hope is for naught.

"Puche binna chale ja rahe hain? Nalayak! You think you can just leave without my permission?" Their father's voice rises, and they know that soon, there will be no calming him. That in this moment of time, there is still a chance to leave here without leaving wreckage in their wake. But the moment is slipping with every word.

"It was all very last-minute. Niklaus invited us with him to Chicago," Dev says, quickly trying to de-escalate the situation, even if it means pinning it on the boy he not-so-secretly loves.

Their father takes a moment with this new information, and the boys are hopeful it will be enough for him to move out of the doorway and let them pass through.

"You're not going. That boy will not use you as charity, to be his lackeys for a day."

"It's not charity. This is Nik. He's not like that," Dev says through gritted teeth.

"You think he views you as equals? That you're anything more than the Indian gardener's sons to him?"

"We're going," Dev says, and he pulls back his shoulders and stands tall, taller than their father, the both of them. But bravado has never worked with their father. He storms his sons, his hands already moving to grab ahold of a collar, to spit some sense into their faces, but they are not the young boys they once were, cowering in fear at the first hint of violence.

Today, Ravi finds his own.

He steps in front of his brother, winds his fist back, and swings. It lands on his father's jaw with a thud, and Ravi winces on impact, his knuckles throbbing. He'd fought before, as a young boy, but he had never meant it, not really. His young fists never carried an overwhelming sense of anger and resentment the way they do now. He takes eighteen years' worth of contempt and slams it into his father's face.

The man stumbles back but doesn't fall. Instead, he holds his face and stares at Ravi, shock turning to anger, glaring now as his jaw reddens.

He opens his mouth, but before either of them can hear what he has to say, Ravi says, "No." He grabs his bag and walks out. Dev quickly shuffles behind him. Neither looks back until they've reached the back door of Rowan Manor, where Nik waits for them. He sits on the grass, studying a leaf, taking note of the way the veins spread across its surface, the way the sunlight creates a perfect shade of green. He doesn't notice them until both boys are looming over him, blocking all the light.

"Shall we?" he says, smiling at them. Dev holds out his hand and Nik grabs it, using him to stand.

"Thanks," Nik says softly. For a moment, Nik grips his hand harder than Dev expects. Nik's eyes are closed, his breathing shallow. But just as quickly as it had come, it passes. Dev's furrowed brow, his quirked head, asks a question. Nik only smiles and shakes his head. Neither lets go until Ravi turns and leads the way, his quick pace urgent. Their father may be stunned one of them stood up to him, but the shock could wear off any minute, and they don't need a repeat of what had happened in front of Nik.

They step into the horse carriage Nik has prepared and begin the quick journey to the train station. There, what comes next will be waiting for them. And though they don't know what it could mean or what's in store, a wave of trepidatious excitement rolls through the three. All have a simmering feeling that things will never be the same again.

Chapter 13

Dev is quiet as they walk back. She sneaks a glance at his ruffled hair and possibly broken nose. His shoulders are hunched, and though he's looking forward, he seems to be lost in thought, staring off into more than just distance.

It's difficult to fathom that just yesterday, Mae was concerned about something as small as telling her parents she doesn't want to go to college just yet. That all she really wants is to spend the year in Chicago figuring herself out, whoever that is. She smiles. The past thirty-six hours have at least put things into perspective. Maybe that conversation wouldn't be so bad. Maybe she is brave enough to have it.

The memory of getting her first sketchbook comes to mind. It was a year before Inez moved to New York. They had spent the afternoon walking around the Everhart Museum, a place that had managed to squeeze natural history and science and art all under one small roof. She'd loved all of it, but it was the art that made her stop in her tracks. The paintings that had her standing there, studying every detail, every brushstroke, for what felt like hours. Inez, an amateur art history fanatic even then, explained the techniques to Mae, the different art periods and movements. She dove into the rich history with such passion and fervor that it felt contagious. Seeing the way Inez lit up when she talked about it, how could Mae not fall in love with art too? When Mae asked Inez if she'd buy her a sketchbook from the gift shop, she didn't hesitate. Mae was an artist because one day Inez showed her beautiful art and Mae wanted to impress her by doing the same. It was as simple as that.

She'd rushed home, looked up YouTube videos on how to draw, and dove right in. The days that followed were more of the same. Back then, her parents didn't care how she spent her time. She was allowed to be a kid, expected to be a kid. But once Inez moved out, it was always school and grades and honor roll and college. In their eyes, there was no room for frivolous art. For wasting time she could have spent studying. Here was their chance for a fresh start after all that had gone wrong with Inez, a daughter that was not welcome back. Mae didn't mind pushing against that, had no problem being the problem. Her grades were fine, there were boys she dated without their knowledge, a friend group she enjoyed. She'd found a way to live with the extra attention they had to give now that it was just her.

But then Inez went missing and the air shifted. Suddenly home became a fragile place, her parents along with it. For months, she's kept the peace, believing that if there is even a small chance that she could save their marriage, it is her responsibility to. It is only now dawning on her that maybe it doesn't have to be this way. That maybe it isn't up to her. Maybe they need to figure their own shit out, and she can stop walking on eggshells around them, worried that she will be the one to finally, irreparably, set them off.

She looks over at Dev and knows he's partly to thank for this shift in her. And even though they're in the middle of nowhere with nothing to their name, she's glad it's him she's stranded with.

"What about your leg?" she says, pulling him out of whatever thought he is in.

"What about it?"

"Shouldn't it heal? Shouldn't you be perfectly healthy?"

"I had this knee injury when the deal was made. This is the body I'm trapped in, the moment in time I keep coming back to," he says softly. He looks down at the silver rabbit head. "The cane helps."

"You're around the age you made the deal," she says, her brow furrowed. It isn't a question.

"Yes?"

"So, when did you last reset?"

He hears the question beneath and shakes his head. "Before she disappeared. Before I got the painting back last year. Someone was sacrificed around the time Ava sold the painting and right before I bought it from Henry." He says it quickly, assuaging her panic before it has time to set in. "Ravi isn't always involved. Usually, he chooses the people, hopes they'll do the hard part on their own, and they usually do. It's human nature to want to pull it back and see what's beneath. But sometimes people find the painting instead of the other way around."

Mae doesn't know what to say to that, mostly relieved that her brief epiphany wasn't much of one. And so they amble toward the parking lot in silence, and there, they see it. The green Jeep Gladiator is a beast next to the sedans it's parked by. Mud splatters mark the bottom edge of the truck, and a New York license plate hangs on the end. Mae pulls on the door handle, but it's locked. No matter. The driver's window is half-open, and so she turns to Dev for help.

"Nothing in the truck bed," he says as he comes around from the back.

"Lift me," she says, opening her arms wide.

"What?" His eyes go wide.

"Lift. Me. I need to get inside and the door is locked."

He stares at the half-open window and then back at Mae, unsure how to proceed. Dev rests his cane against the green paint of the truck and comes up behind her, gently placing his hands on her waist. For a second, neither of them moves. The only sound is their breathing and the warm wind that whips through their hair. She can feel the heat of his hands through the thin fabric and reminds herself to breathe. Painting first, immortal sad boys later.

"Priorities," she mumbles to herself, and jumps. His hands grip her waist as she uses the edge of the window as leverage. She stretches, reaching for the unlock button, and, once they both hear it click, jumps down. He doesn't let go immediately.

She busies herself by opening the door and jumping inside, and he goes around to the passenger side and climbs in.

Inside, it is pristine. Ravi hasn't left much for them to go through. Mae rummages through the side compartment between the seats and pulls out three passports.

She looks up to find Dev holding four bound stacks of hundred-dollar bills. From the glove compartment.

"Holy shit."

"Find anything?" he asks.

She shows him the passports and flips through them. "This is his. This one too, but under a different name. And this is—" She opens the last one and freezes. "Inez. Why does he have Inez's passport?" She looks up at Dev, but he has the same answers she does. In the photo, her sister smiles back. She looks happy. Content.

"Maybe they were going somewhere, maybe she forgot it here?" Dev says, hopeful.

"Maybe." She thinks back to the Polaroid in her sister's notebook, Ravi as he kisses her cheek. They were together at some point. That much is true. So it isn't a leap to think it plausible Inez had simply forgotten her passport in his car.

"Find anything else?" she asks him. She tears her eyes away from Inez's photo but finds that she can't put it back in the compartment and so returns the others and holds this one tight.

He shakes his head. "Back to square one," Dev says as he leans back against the headrest.

"Or not." Mae holds up the car keys Ravi had forgotten in

the cupholder. Her eyes light up as she stares at them and it's then it dawns on her. Losing her phone is a best-case scenario, not worst.

"My phone, I forgot it in the car. We can use Find My Phone to track it."

"And Ravi." They look at each other as grins break out on their faces. Maybe this isn't a dead end after all. She goes to start the car, but Dev stretches out his hand for the keys. She narrows her eyes at him but doesn't argue. She'd rather be riding shotgun anyway. They get out and switch sides, walking past each other, the shining headlights outlining them for a brief moment before they're back inside and ready to go.

Dev reverses out of the spot, and he's out of there before Mae can even buckle her seat belt.

She pulls up the app on his phone and there, miles away, past Canada and in Vermont, is her phone. But at the sight of the border on the map, she realizes the obvious.

"Dev, I don't have my ID." Her eyes are wide in sheer panic, but he looks down at her hand gripping her sister's passport. He doesn't even hesitate.

"What? No, I can't. I don't even look anything like her." The less logical answer is that it just feels wrong.

"Do you have any better ideas?"

She doesn't, and so she sighs and agrees. What choice does she have? She pulls up the app again and directs him back to the highway. The dot is racing forward, and within minutes, they are too. Eventually, they reach the American border, and it dawns on Mae, if it wasn't bad enough that she's using identification that isn't hers, they're in a car that isn't theirs with a suspicious amount of cash in the glove compartment.

"You don't think they'd search us, do you?" she says as Dev slowly inches forward in the customs line. "The money is already suspicious, but we have no idea what he has in here. What if we missed something?"

"Let's just not give them a reason to." He slows to a stop as he reaches the officer and, after a suspicious amount of time spent looking for the button, slides the window down.

"Hello, Officer," Dev says a little too cheerily for Mae's liking.

"IDs."

"Sure thing." He hands them over, and they wait while he inspects them.

"Are you bringing anything back with you?"

"Nope." Mae can see he's eager to get going, that every minute spent here is a minute Ravi races ahead of them, but his answer, though true, is too quick.

The officer eyes them both, his eyes landing on Dev and back again as he compares the Dev on the ID with the one in the car. It's her she expects to be the problem, but for some reason, all the officer has done is throw a quick glance her way. He pockets the ID and passport and walks away without saying a word.

"What just happened?" Mae whispers. She doesn't know if it's possible to be arrested by border control, but of course, it's the only place her mind will go. "Are my parents going to have to bail me out of jail?"

"Unlikely. Just give him a minute," he whispers back.

Eventually the man comes back but with a second officer, their flashlights ready and beaming. One focuses on the truck bed, making sure to check every corner even though Mae is almost sure it's empty. The other she catches from the side mirror, checking beneath the car, feeling around for any hidden compartments.

"What are the odds your brother is a drug lord?" she asks, half-serious.

"He'd be too smart to use his own car." She doesn't think he's kidding.

"Okay, you're free to go," the officer says, handing Dev the ID and passport.

The bar isn't even fully raised before Dev has floored it out of there. Mae turns to see the two uniformed officers pointing their flashlights their way, one shaking his head. Dev sets Inez's passport and his ID in the cupholder, and Mae grabs his, studying the photo. The Dev here is older than the one she knows, in his forties with graying hair at his temples. No wonder the officer was suspicious. But it is a strange thing to see a photo of the future, to time travel forward as she sits in place. If she never knows him then, she thinks, she'll always have this glimpse into who that would have been.

She pulls up the app again and spends the next while giving him directions, but soon enough the directions stop. The little dot doesn't move any farther, and they get closer and closer until they miss it entirely. There aren't any other drivers on the road, and yet, there is no Ravi waiting for them. Dev parks on the side of the road and they both get out.

The phone must be there, why else would it lead them here? She calls herself on Dev's phone, and in the distance, there is a ringing, a soft sound muffled by the dirt and tall grass a few feet away from the empty road. Dev looks at her, his eyes alert, before he disappears inside the dark expanse. She waits and listens, both for the phone and for Dev. When she can only hear Dev moving through the grass, she calls her number again and guides him to the phone. Eventually he comes back, phone in hand. Her heart sinks: Finding the phone means losing Ravi, and she is tired of dead ends. From the way Dev's free hand is in a tight fist, she isn't the only one. He returns it to her and walks away as he weaves his fingers behind his neck and stares up into the dark, star-smattered sky. There is nothing for them to do. With their one connection to Ravi gone, they are aimless and they know it.

"Wait. Where are we?" Dev asks. He walks over to where she's standing near the car.

Mae looks for the nearest sign. When there isn't one, she pulls up the maps app on her phone.

"I-89, still in Vermont, between Highgate and Fairfield."

"No." But he says it softly, almost afraid she's right.

He looks down the road, like he could see the end of it if only he squinted hard enough. He doesn't look at her, only off into the distance as he leans against the car. His forehead rests on the edge of the open window and she waits for him to say something. Anything.

"You know where he is." It isn't a question. He nods and, after a second, walks over to the driver's side and climbs inside.

She follows suit, and seconds later the car is going eighty miles an hour.

"Do I get to know where we're going, or is it a surprise?" she says into the silence.

"I grew up an hour from here. In Montpelier, Vermont. He's there. He has to be."

"Like one hundred thirty-three years ago grew up?"

He nods.

Mae pulls up the map and zooms out. She scrolls down, her finger following the interstate south, in the direction he's looking, curving with it until she stops miles away from where they are. Montpelier, just like he said

"What if we're walking into a trap? What if he knew you'd see through this, him throwing the phone away, and that you'd connect the dots about where he was going next. What if he wants to settle this? Once and for all." There is panic in her voice, she hears it, but Dev is complete calm as he shakes his head.

"Good. For once, we want the same thing." He presses his foot against the pedal and races toward certain demise.

Home.

Chapter 14

Nik has reserved a cabin for them. The long terra-cotta velvet seats and dark mahogany wood that covers the walls and floor make the space feel intimate. A large window occupies one wall, and Dev watches as green pastures roll by far too fast. He's never been on a train before, never knew of the rumble beneath his feet or the heat against his face. Moments like these, Dev cannot deny he enjoys being in Nik's world, even if he lives on its edges. Ravi has left to wander, and Nik and Dev are alone. It is often the three of them, but Dev's heart beats differently when they are left to themselves, not faster or slower, but sweeter. Warmer.

Dev notices Nik has pinned the leaf from earlier to the sketchbook page, their train tickets shoved in the middle of empty pages like makeshift bookmarks. He's only a quarter into this one. Dev had loved poring over his last one, studying the detail and color of pages Nik spent years putting together. But his parents had never been supportive of his botany dreams, or his gentle soul to be honest, and had thrown it in the fire before Nik could stop them. They'd said it had made him too delicate, too weak. He remembered finding Nik in the garden one late night last May, crying in the dark. The clouds had covered the moon and Dev had nearly missed him, but Dev had always gravitated toward Nik. He could always find him in a room, could almost sense him near. It was possible that Dev was in fact always looking for Nik, that a part of him was constantly reaching forward.

Dev had found him that night and needed to pull the truth out of him. Nik had smiled through tear-streaked cheeks and tried to convince Dev it was nothing.

"Niklaus," Dev said, and it was all it took for the story to pour out. Dev had wanted so badly to march into Rowan Manor, collect the ashes of Nik's most prized possession, and shape them into something recognizable again. But all he could do was listen.

"They said it was time I grew out of this hobby, that it had made me . . . too soft." His voice broke when he said it, and Dev wrapped his arms around him as Nik tried his best to collect himself. Nik had one arm wrapped around Dev's waist, the other against the back of his neck. Nik should have been the one being comforted, but it was Dev who felt safe in his embrace. Nik eventually stepped away, took a deep breath.

"They can burn this, the sketchbook, the charcoal, but they can't take it," Dev said. "Not truly, anyway." He'd taken hold of Nik's face, making sure that he had his full attention. He remembers now how warm his cheeks were, still damp from his tears. "It will always be yours," Dev told him. Nik smiled at Dev's words even if he didn't quite believe them. Not yet, anyway.

That night, they went their separate ways to their separate homes. Dev couldn't stop thinking about the way Nik's parents had broken a part of him and just how badly he wanted to mend it. At dawn, he pulled back the rug in his bedroom, lifted the loose floorboard beneath, and took a few bills from the pile. Ravi was still asleep, but Dev knew Ravi wouldn't argue with this. Nik was deserving of much more than either of them could give.

He stood in front of the art supplies shop, waiting for the owner to arrive. Finally, the door opened to him and he stepped inside. He wandered down the aisles as he slowly scanned the shelves. Everything here felt so lavish, so fragile. Yet, he couldn't help but run his fingers through the silky horsehair brushes, the thick cold-pressed paper, and smooth, hollow canvases. He squeezed the edge of a tube of green oil paint, denting the thin metal surface, and moved to the next aisle before anyone saw him.

There, he found it. A beautiful brown leather-bound book, soft and heavy in his hands. It was small enough to tuck into a pocket, discreet. Dev paid for it, along with a pack of charcoal and a few pencils of the same brand he'd noticed Nik carrying around, and made the long walk back to Rowan Manor. He went through the back door, usually left open, and when a maid saw him, he raised a finger to his lips and pointed up to Nik's room. She shook her head and pursed her lips but continued wiping the dining table. It wasn't the first time she'd caught Dev sneaking in. He made his way around the corner, to the stairwell, and up to Nik's bedroom, where he'd only now just woken up.

Nik stirred at the sight of Dev's silhouette in his doorway. Dev stepped into his room and, on the bed, placed the book, pencils, and charcoal he had snuck in his pocket. Nik grinned at the sight of it all, lost for words. Before he could thank him, Dev said, "This is for you. I—I have to go."

He rushed off, leaving Nik alone with the small book in his lap. Dev couldn't bear to be there when Nik flipped through it to find a lily pressed between two pages. Beneath it, Dev's neat, clean handwriting. *Soft as you, and just as beautiful.*

On the train, fields rush past them. Sun shines through the small cabin that feels much smaller than it is with just Nik and Dev inside. Once Ravi returns, it will somehow feel bigger, but until then, there is nowhere Dev can look that he doesn't feel Nik's gaze, feel his presence, see his long body, which is now inconveniently stretched out across the length of the cabin, his black boots resting against Dev's thigh, the heel crinkling the newspaper beneath it. He tries his best to focus on anything else. On the loose thread at the edge of the velvet seat, on the streak of dusty light shining against the hardwood floor. The mark on the wall near Nik's face. But that's a bad idea because he's now just rounded back to studying Nik's face as he sketches the leaf. His auburn hair shines in the sunlight as one strand falls toward his face. He doesn't move it, too focused on the page as he is. Nik's cheeks are eternally rosy, though Dev especially loves the winters when Nik's rosy cheeks spread and he carries a blush anytime the cold blows onto his face. His white sweater falls against his chest in a way that forces Dev to look away. But it's too late. Nik looks up and sees him staring.

Nik doesn't mention it, only turns his face, hiding the hint of a smile.

Dev senses that Nik has been different as of late. In the way he holds his gaze a second longer than usual, the way his arm brushes past Dev's, lingering. Even now as Nik's boot touches Dev's thigh, he doesn't know what to make of this bolder Nik. If he's reading too much into it or if Nik is telling him something the best way he can and Dev only need listen. He can't recall when it happened, the moment his feelings shifted, but thinks he's always loved him. There is no other way to be.

If it wasn't for Nik and Ravi, Dev would have spent a childhood alone. He never felt like the kids at school. Too brown, too foreign, too strange. He was a feather among stones and no one let him forget it. Except for Nik and Ravi. The three had been friends as soon as the boys were old enough to wander the grounds unchaperoned, well before things like *class* and *propriety* could have stood in their way. As soon as they found each other at the edge of the Wildwood.

It was Dev who came across Nik in the speckled light. Nik was lifting rocks to let the bugs roam free, not knowing they had sought out those very rocks, that he was only taking homes, not doing favors.

"Hi," Dev said, and Nik smiled up at him. He handed Dev a rock, and they spent all afternoon beneath the netted shade of oak trees, searching underneath every stone for insects in need of rescuing.

Eventually, Dev's mother had found them in the dirt, their knees muddy and clothes stained. Back then, she was healthy, happy. Full of life she was empty of now. When the illness came years later, it ravaged her in mere months. There was no stopping it.

Dev does what he always does when his thoughts go to his mother. He studies his hands and quickly checks for tremors, the first of her symptoms. It's as if he's pulled out of his body in these brief moments, always watching from a distance in case this is it. He holds them low, so Nik doesn't notice, but they're steady, as always. The quick surge of fear passes, and Dev finds himself back in his body, rooted in this train, this cabin, this seat, across from the boy he loves. *I am all right*, he thinks to himself. *I'm here. With Nik. What more could I want?*

He glances up and catches Nik's eye. They both look away, as Dev pretends not to notice being sketched. He wonders what Nik sees, wants to ask what details his charcoal lingers on. If these answers mean something more. Instead, Dev rests his head against the glass, closes his eyes, and listens as Nik's charcoal glides across the page.

An Interlude

*A*nthony Mason *cannot explain why he is drawn to* The White Expanse. *What is it about its spare canvas and curling corner that tugs at him? Why can't he look away? In all honesty, Anthony would pay any number to make it his, so when the gallery owner mentions the price, there is not a moment's hesitation in Anthony's eyes.*

The gallerist notices, regretting not going higher. How much would this man have paid? *he wonders. The gallerist calls to his assistant, who takes it down from where it hangs on the wall. She carefully wraps it for Anthony, making sure to be gentle with its fragile frame. The gold foil has already begun to chip in the corners.*

Anthony speeds home, the painting sitting in the back seat, blocking his rear window for the entire six hours and eleven minutes. He turns into his driveway too quickly and haphazardly parks in front of the large house. Anthony gently pulls the painting out of the back seat and takes it inside to his office, where a blank wall waits. He sets it down on the floor and tears

at the thick brown paper tightly wrapped around it in a frenzy.
He smiles as his eyes meet that familiar abyss once again.

His wife comes into the room as he hammers two nails into
the wall, tearing the olive-green wallpaper she had handpicked
herself. Ava clenches her jaw and glares at her husband's new
painting. It's blank. Large, sure, but even the frame is more
beautiful than anything she can find on that empty canvas.
She doesn't ask how much he paid for this one. She knows not
to. There is always money for the things she needs, wants, and
until that changes, he can have his toys, she thinks to herself.
Better spent on things than affairs. She minds this much less
than the Jenny and Jim and Jamie he's run around with in the
past. Inevitably there would be someone else. But for now—
well, for now he can do as he pleases if it's only with the wall.

He doesn't notice as she watches him from the doorway. He
is too fixated on the task at hand.

In the coming weeks, Anthony will sit at his desk for hours
on end and stare at that vast canvas, study its gold frame, its
smooth texture and swirling brushstrokes. He will spend two
months doing this.

And then one day, on an afternoon not unlike this one, he
will stop.

Chapter 15

Nik uses the edge of his thumb to smooth out an area he had patiently shaded and goes back with his charcoal to better define it. Away from home and with no reason to hide it, he is enjoying the mess the charcoals make on his hands, the page, his pockets. They smudge the tips of his fingers, the pad of his palm, and he happily lets them.

"What's caught your eye?" Dev finally asks as he often does when he sees Nik working away in a sketchbook. They are alone in the cabin, Ravi off still wandering the train, his book in hand when he left, and Dev's voice sounds tender in the space between them, tenuous. There is a roughness to his almost whisper that makes Nik look up.

His eyebrows shoot up as he looks at Dev and back down to the page. He cannot think of a more vulnerable thing than to answer Dev's question with a portrait of Dev.

"Nothing of note," Nik says, quickly closing the sketchbook and putting it to the side.

"I'm going to stretch my legs, need anything?" Nik asks.

He stands as Dev shakes his head. But it's too abrupt of

a move and the world spins around him. He feels the weight of himself held by weak knees. Around him, the edges of the cabin glow white, too bright to make out.

"Nik?" Dev says, and his hands are suddenly around his waist, firm around his elbow. "Nik." He says it again, but it sounds muffled in Nik's ears, far away. Dev guides him back to his seat and sits with him as Nik takes a minute to steady his heartbeat, to steady the world around him. In the quiet, he can hear his thudding heart laboring to pump blood quickly enough.

"Are you okay? You're looking a bit peaked," Dev says.

He knows there is a sheen to his pale face, that his breath comes short and quick. He could tell him the truth right then and there, even considers it for a moment, but the words don't come. They live somewhere deep inside him, and right now, they are too far to reach.

Nik nods and smiles. "Just stood too quickly is all. I'm okay. I promise."

He reaches forward and squeezes Dev's knee, a thumb on his thigh. He feels like a liar. Every time he touches him, he feels like a liar. And yet, he reaches anyway. Keeps reaching.

Dev doesn't look convinced, but this time, Nik walks away before he can ask anything else. He slides the door shut behind him.

Along the corridor and through a set of doorways is the entrance to the food cart, and there at the end, he finds Ravi stretched out in a booth with a book in his hands. He smiles at the page for a moment and flips it quickly, eager to get to the next part.

"What are you reading?" Nik asks as he sits across from him.

Ravi answers his question with a question. "Have you told him yet?"

Nik ignores him. He'd much rather talk about Ravi's book.

"*The Picture of Dorian Gray*," he says, reading the title on the cover. "Any good?"

Ravi shuts the book and moves it to the side. His full attention on Nik.

"Have you told him?" he asks again.

"Not yet, must have slipped my mind," Nik says, picking at the edge of his thumb. He can feel Ravi's gaze on him.

"Nik," he says firmly, and here he finally looks up.

"Ravi."

There is silence between them as they stare at each other, waiting for the other to break.

"Maybe I never have to tell him," Nik says. A smile plays on his lips, but it is half-hearted at best.

Ravi sighs. "I agreed to go on this ridiculous journey for you. Because I knew you wanted this last adventure with him. But you must tell him."

"I'd rather just have the adventure," Nik mumbles, picking at the splintered edge of the table.

"They're sending you away. What will you tell him then? That you've signed on for the army, that you'll write to him when time permits? You'll break his heart."

"It's better than *Dev, I'm dying and there is little to be done about it*." The smile is gone now. No use pretending. "My heart

is failing, Ravi. It's failing, and I'm not ready to say goodbye."
Ravi reaches a hand forward and places it on top of Nik's. He
can feel the worry radiating from Ravi's very core.

"I can only imagine how hard this is on you. I'm sorry."

"Don't be. You're right. I owe him this. I want him to know.
I want you both to know. I'm not sure why I told you first, I'm
just sorry I've pulled you into all this secrecy with me."

Ravi studies Nik for a few seconds. He opens his mouth,
then closes it again. The words don't seem to be forming just
right.

Finally, "You told me first because it was easier, because
what you share with Dev has always been different than what
you and I share."

"That's not tr—" Nik begins, cutting him off, but Ravi lifts a
hand, asking for Nik to let him continue. Nik nods.

"I see the way you both look at each other. I know my
brother." And after a moment, "I know you. And neither of you
are as subtle as you think."

Nik says nothing, but he does not deny it. He thinks of all
the stolen glances and brushed hands. The flushed cheeks and
lingering smiles, all in sight of Ravi.

"If you were hiding your affections or holding back on my
account, don't. I've always loved you two just the same."

Nik smiles.

"Personally, I'll never understand why it's my brother you're
fond of, but the heart wants what it wants," Ravi says with a
wink. And with that, he opens his book and begins to read
again. Nik knows it's a kind gesture. One that does not force

Nik into admitting or denying anything he does not want to. One that lets Nik decide how much or how little to say. He is reminded of just how much he loves Ravi, how he has always seen a brother in him.

"I see."

Nik jumps at the sound of Dev's voice over his shoulder.

"I come to check on you and find you much prefer Ravi's company over mine. It's unforgiveable, really," Dev says as he slides into the booth next to Ravi.

"Can you blame him?" Ravi says without looking away from his book. Dev ignores him and nudges Nik's foot with his own beneath the table. Keeps it there, ankle against ankle, knees brushing, neither moving.

"You okay?" Dev asks softly.

"Much better."

Ravi looks up from his page and quirks an eyebrow.

"I just stood too quickly. Feeling much better now."

Ravi squints at him, just barely. If he wasn't looking for it, he might have missed the tiny nod in Dev's direction. *Here is an opening*, he tells him. But the thought of uttering the words aloud to Dev leaves Nik's stomach in knots, and he'd much rather talk about anything else than his own impending demise.

Just then a woman with a coffee cart ambles by, and Nik stops her to order three coffees for them. Ravi opens his mouth to protest, but Nik waves him off. "I got it," he says, and pays the woman with the coins in his pocket. She sets down three steaming cups, and the scent of fresh-brewed coffee surrounds them.

"What do you think waits for us in Chicago?" Nik asks as he takes a sip. The cup instantly warms his pallid hands.

"Nothing. I'm here to make sure you two get back in one piece." Ravi's returned to his book now, one arm over the booth, the other holding a page in place. He stares at his cup of coffee for a moment but doesn't touch it.

"And for an *I told you so* if we leave Chicago empty-handed," Dev throws back.

"I don't need to say it for you to know it's true."

Nik is used to the brothers' bickering. By now, he knows better than to come in the way of it; they will lose steam eventually. He's left his sketchbook in the cabin, but he spots a newspaper someone has discarded in the booth to his left and grabs it. In his pocket is a broken piece of charcoal, the end dull but workable. In the margins of the newspaper, he sketches out the two brothers across from him. Ravi's relaxed arm over the booth, the book in his hand. His eyes are focused on the pages even though he responds to Dev, whose annoyance is clear as day in his tight shoulders, his heated face. He always lets his brother get under his skin, always lets him pick him apart. He can see how it bothers Dev, how he finds it impossible to let it go. He needs the last word, and Ravi has too easy of a time getting it.

His thoughts return to Chicago and Delphine Lefroy's painting. He wonders what it could mean for him. For all of them.

Anything they could want. He knows there will be a price to pay, something the woman made of shadows will need in return, but Nik is optimism personified. If the woman needs something from them, they will deal with it then. They will figure it out together. There's no use worrying over what they have no control over. Wondering what he would ask, though, is a much more fun exercise. Her words were this: *Find it and what you seek most shall find you.*

With that, Nik hears the thudding of a solid, rhythmic heartbeat. He hears not having to be sent away because his parents no longer want to deal with him or his erratic heart. He hears reprieve. For as long as he can remember, Nik has only disappointed his family. Too weak, too fragile, too sensitive, he shares no resemblance to the man his father so desperately wants him to be, the son his mother hoped for. How can he, when he too readily follows every soft whim he desires?

He wonders what the woman's words mean to the Sharma brothers. He studies them as they sit across from him. Ravi, if he had to guess, hears wealth. Endless prosperity and good fortune. He would not fault him for it. The twins have lived a difficult life, and Ravi has always been practical. Rational. Nik is not so obtuse to his own good fortune that he is not aware money does indeed fix many of life's problems.

Nik looks over to Dev and finds himself unsure. He knows Dev, knows him like the back of his charcoal-smudged hand, but this answer doesn't come as readily. There is a brief, thrilling moment where Nik wonders if it's him, that if Dev were to know the truth about his stuttering heart, the thing he'd want most in this world would be to save him.

But he doesn't let the thought settle. It's too fragile a hope, too heavy a want. He moves on, thinks of something, anything else.

In the back of his mind though, the thought takes root.

Chapter 16

The boys gather their things as the train comes to a stop at Pittsburgh Station. They are almost halfway to Chicago, but another train will have to take them the rest of the way, and so they follow Ravi out to the platform. Passengers rush out and lug their suitcases and bags through the cold rain, in a rush to get home, warm and dry. A few huddle beneath the awning to transfer to the next train as theirs lurches forward without them. The sound of rain thrumming against the overhang reverberates across the station.

"It should be here in an hour or so," Ravi says as he checks the train schedule taped to the green awning post.

"Plenty of time for food; we should be able to find a hot meal close by."

"Actually," Ravi begins, thinking of the sandwiches he had packed for them in his bag. But Dev jumps in before he has a chance to finish the thought.

"Let's. I'm famished."

Ravi considers telling them about the food he's already prepared, but his face warms at the thought. He knows the bread is stale by now, the spread too warm to be all that appetizing. He lets them walk ahead of him before quickly opening his bag to throw out the wrapped sandwiches that sit atop his things, dropping them into the metal trash can. He stares at the discarded food and can't seem to muster up any of the tender care he held for it last night.

A few minutes later, they're sitting in a corner of a dim tavern surrounded by the chatter of patrons. Near them, a fire crackles and the heat of it is unrelenting. Their table is sticky and small, but minutes ago they were running through rain-slicked streets, and so no one complains.

Nik pushes back his wet hair, and Ravi doesn't miss the way Dev watches Nik, his eyes on the persistent strand that makes its way forward. Ravi looks away and thinks of the money tucked in his bag. They can afford a meal; it's why they've brought the money. But Ravi doesn't know what this trip will bring, if they'll regret spending any of it here. It's not until the food comes that Ravi realizes how ravenous he is. He tears the warm bread in two and dips it into the beef stew. The tender meat melts in his mouth; the sauce is rich and as seasoned as he's come to expect in this country—enough.

They finish their bowls in record time. Ravi feels fuller than he's been in days.

"Should we get going?" Dev asks.

Nik nods and sets a handful of coins on the table, more than enough to cover the food. Ravi's stomach turns at the sight of it, his food quickly unsettling.

"You don't have to do that. We can cover our own meals."

"That's all right," Nik says, smiling. "I don't mind." He stands up and puts on his wool coat, oblivious to Ravi's discomfort.

Ravi puts on his still-damp coat and follows them. He wants to push, to fight him until he takes the money back, but this has always been Nik: kind and unaware of the way his wealth has made Ravi feel. On some nights, he can't help but think of his family in another life, the Sharmas with all their affluence and land still. He pinpoints the moment they lost it all, when their father took a gamble on America, and rewinds time. For a few seconds, he pretends things had gone another way. That he is in India with more money than he can ever know what to do with. It is a life where Ravi never has to work and tire and scheme to reclaim his family's status because they never lost it to begin with.

Here, he doesn't have to hold on to bitter memories of watching his father use up every dollar they had until he was forced to take the only job he could find, a gardener's apprentice on the Rowan estate, a job he'd known nothing of but had put his all into until there was nothing left of him for Ravi and Dev, for their mother. Long days beneath the blistering sun as he planted and pruned until his hands were rough and calloused. His father has had dirt beneath his fingernails for longer than Ravi's known him without.

Ravi stuffs his hands into threadbare pockets to fight the brisk wind as they make their way back to the train station. The thick strap of his bag digs into his shoulder all the way there.

By the time they reach the station, a crowd has gathered on

the platform. The rain has stopped, only a mist now, and soon enough their train rumbles onto the tracks.

It comes to a halt in front of them, and the boys join the line of people making their way in. Dev and Nik talk in front of Ravi but he doesn't have it in him to join in, and so he stays quiet. He doesn't think they notice.

They make their way inside the car, and he follows along as Nik leads them to their cabin. It's more crowded than he expects, and passengers surge past him. He lets them, finds himself in no rush to join the other two.

"You, there," a voice says. A rough hand lands on his shoulder and tugs him back before he has a chance to turn. "Ticket."

The conductor glowers at him, and all Ravi can do is stare back helplessly. He thinks of Nik with all their train tickets tucked into his sketchbook, a car between them now.

"My friend has my ticket. I just need to find him," he says, pointing over his shoulder.

The man shakes his head and grips the edge of his coat. "Nice try," he says as he begins to pull Ravi toward the open doors.

"I'm not lying. I have a ticket," Ravi says, pulling against him, but the man only holds his coat tighter, tearing the seams along the shoulder. The conductor's other hand strikes his back and shoves him forward.

There's a second where Ravi notes the eyes on him: the so-called gentlefolk in the first-class car, the people who look away and the ones who laugh as Ravi is dragged toward the doors. He has never been so aware of his brown skin, the way it beckons their gaze.

"Wait!" a voice yells out.

Ravi and the conductor turn to find Nik running toward them. He's breathing hard and waving his sketchbook in the air as if it's all the proof they need Ravi belongs here.

"He's with me, I have his ticket right here," Nik says between gulps of air, but before he can even pull it out, the conductor has released Ravi from his firm grip, Nik's fair skin and expensive coat the only proof the man needed.

"Your lucky day, son," he says gruffly, and shoves past them. The onlookers move on just as quickly.

"You okay?" Nik asks, his face flushed. He puts a hand on Ravi's shoulder, but he shrugs him off.

"I had it handled," Ravi says, looking away.

Nik's brow furrows. His eyes are wide in shock. "Handled? Ravi, he was about to throw you off. I was just trying to help."

Ravi finds it difficult to hold on to logic. Nik *did* have his train ticket, after all. Instead, all Ravi can think of is how the conductor never needed to look at it; just one glance at Niklaus Rowan and suddenly, his word would overpower Ravi's every time. Ravi does not belong to him, is not his to save, and yet, why is it so difficult to believe otherwise? My God, he is so tired of feeling powerless.

"I'm not your charity case," Ravi says, repeating the echo in his head. His father's voice has never had trouble burrowing into him.

"I know," Nik says, and the hurt drips from every word. "You're my friend."

Ravi looks back at him, silent, and regret fills him just as quickly as he had lashed out. Why does he have to lead with pride? Why can't he understand it isn't Nik's fault the world is stacked against Ravi?

Ravi sighs. "I apologize. I—I shouldn't have said that." He doesn't wait for Nik to respond. Instead, he moves past him and goes to find his brother, leaving Nik behind.

Last December

Inez waits alone at the bar. She nurses a whiskey, neat, and glances at her phone. He's fifteen minutes late now, and though she usually doesn't mind, tonight is different. Her boot taps the edge of the stool as she watches the door, willing him to walk through it.

And then he does.

Ravi unwinds his red scarf and shakes off the snow from his buzzed hair. When his eyes meet hers, he grins.

When she beams back, it is instinct, her body reacting before her mind can remind her that, soon enough, his smile will no longer be hers.

"Hi, love," he says. He bends to kiss her and she turns, giving him her cheek.

"We need to talk," she says softly. She clears her throat and sits up straight, faking the confidence that won't yet come.

"No *Hi. How are you, Ravi? How was your day?*" He quirks his head. The edge of a smirk pulls at his lips.

"I can't do this anymore."

"Do what?" Ravi asks as he waves toward the bartender. He

points at her drink and motions for another. Finally, he swivels on his stool and faces her. It's only now, with his full attention on Inez, that he notices her impassive expression. Her inscrutable gaze.

"Do what, Inez?" His smile falls, and she knows he is beginning to understand.

"This. You and me," she says, gesturing to him and back as if what they have lives in the space between. He reels back like he has been struck by the force of her words.

"What are you talking about?"

"Dev won't give me the painting. And that's fine because I'm done being used."

"Used? I've never—that's not what I—" He stops and starts again. "This was our plan. Together. I thought it was what you wanted. I didn't know you felt this way."

"I thought I wouldn't eventually. But I've felt like this for a while."

"Inez, we're so close," he pleads, holding her hands.

"Is it me you're worried about losing, or the painting?" she spits, and he flinches.

"You. Of course, it's you," he says, shaking his head. "I'm sorry, I shouldn't have—forget it. Forget all of it."

"It's too late for that. I'm done," she says as she pulls her hands away from his. He slumps, and it's as if she's taken something of him with her.

"But I—I love you." And it's all he can think to say.

Her eyes are locked on his. "I don't. Not anymore." She doesn't waver when she says it. She needs him to understand.

She won't leave here and have him doubt her, can't have a single part of him, no matter how small, suspect the truth.

Her coat, bag, are already in hand when she stands. She doesn't turn as she makes her way through the crowded bar. Just takes one step after the next until she's standing in the cold, snow piling around her as it muffles the city into an eerie stillness. It lands in her hair, atop her sweater, and she lets it. She doesn't notice she's crying until the biting wind smarts her tear-streaked cheeks. Inez takes a deep breath, crisp in her lungs, wipes her face, and makes her way toward the Union Square subway station, her footprints making small indents in the building snow behind her.

Recently, dread had been blooming in her stomach, replaying this moment on a loop before it even happened, but there is no other way for this to go. She was always going to break his heart, and her own. It is a sacrifice she is willing to make. Inez refuses to lose sight of her own plan. Not this close to the end. He will forget her in time, and if she's lucky, she will too. By the time she's home, her footprints are lost to the snowfall.

Chapter 17

N ik is the one to see it first.

He knows something looks off, strange. He does not know why it feels unnatural, just that it does. This train cabin is a puzzle, and he looks around trying to find an answer. And then it clicks. If he were to reach for the soft leather of the sketchbook tucked into his back pocket and draw Ravi and Dev sleeping across from him, he would shape their forms, delicately draw Dev's head against Ravi's shoulder, the way their long bodies are splayed out, their legs a jumble on the floor. Then he would add the shadows, create dimension, sketch where the light lands and where it misses them. But Dev and Ravi don't have shadows. Instead, they shine bright, lit in a way that doesn't make sense against the dim overhead light that begins to flicker above them. He studies the bulb, waiting for it to steady. Slowly, he reaches his hand forward, directly below the light. Beneath his hand, a shadow forms, just like it should. But before he can pull it back, the shadow moves before he does.

It retreats away from him, farther and farther away until it pools beneath the sliding door and slips through. Now that he knows what to look for, it is obvious. All around him, the shadows retreat from where they should be, shifting toward the door and disappearing beneath the thin crack at its edge—as if answering something's call. There is a moment of silence, only sliced through by Nik's erratically beating heart.

"Dev, Ravi," he whispers. He kicks their feet and they jump, disoriented for a second before sitting up.

"There's something wrong. Something is happening," Nik says as he looks around, searching for a shadow. He hopes it was all a strange trick of the light, that it's his eyes he can't trust, but everything in the cabin blurs, loses definition as it swims with everything else. The world around him is melting away.

"What's the matter?" Dev asks, concern etched between his brows. Nik opens his mouth to answer, but before he can, he is pulled away in one swift movement. He is a rag doll against a current. The door shoots open and Nik barely has time to scream before he is dragged by nothing, or more accurately, something the others cannot see.

"Nik!" Dev shouts after him. Dev and Ravi are on their feet in less than a second. The brothers share a fleeting look before they see it.

Outside the cabin is only night.

Shadows. Shadows among shadows pooling and roiling in the doorway, they swim against the edges of the doorframe, and then in one quick movement they race toward Ravi and pull him under, dragging him out of the cabin the same way they did Nik.

Dev is alone.

For a moment, he is stunned in the stillness; the only sensation that fills the small space is the thundering train beneath his feet. But quickly he snaps out of his stupor and runs toward the now-retreating shadows. They disappear around the corner and Dev follows, trailing them down the long, narrow hallway.

He finds himself face-to-face with the woman with no name. He pales at the sight of her. She is all edges and corners, the shadows against her face moving like they're playing with an unsteady light source.

"I chose *you*. Sought *you* out," she says, pointing a finger at his chest, her sharp nail digging into his sweater. "This is not their prize to win, their treasure to find. They will go no farther on this journey."

"I'm not leaving them," he says. His voice trembles, but his gaze is unwavering as he watches the shadows dance around her, like a breeze winding its way through. They caress her, move and twist like snakes in search of home.

"Dear boy. What lies ahead is far more treacherous than anything you leave behind. If you cared for them, you would spare them."

He does not know if he should believe her. She has no reason to lie to him. And yet, the thought of doing this alone fills him with such panic, he feels utterly consumed by it. "I won't do this without them. I don't want this without them. Whatever this is."

"Do the others know? That you must all be prepared for the cost? It is steeper than you dare dream," she reminds him.

He doesn't respond, but she bares her teeth in a laugh. It is all the answer she needs.

"Oh, Dev Sharma. You fool." She leans closer, her nail slicing against skin. "To have what you want, you must give all that you have."

Dev's heart beats in his throat. He swallows. Perhaps he should have shared with them the details of what she had said that night in the woods, should have given them a chance to heed her warning, but he had made the decision for them, too afraid they would make the wrong one. There is no going back now. And in all honesty, it does not matter what he'll pay. He will not lose them both, will not abandon them to whatever shadows she has called upon to take them away. Dev cannot do any of this without them. His hands shake, but he grips them into fists and stands firm, refusing to cower under her gaze. He is immovable, and she will know it.

Finally, she steps aside, the dark swarming her once again, and he takes that as the only answer he'll get.

The shadows that had taken Ravi and Nik slither along the walls in fluid, snakelike motions toward the end of the dark hallway, and though he can't see either of them, he knows they are in the dark abyss ahead. He runs blindly into shadows, only the sound of his quick footsteps to guide him. Even the sound of the train feels muffled here, muted. In the distance, there is the hushed whooshing sound of train doors opening. He runs faster now, into the blackness, until finally he sees it, a light at the end in the shape of a door. And there they are, Nik and Ravi, wrapped in shadow, being dragged to its edge. There is a moment, one brief and agonizingly slow moment, where Dev's eyes meet Nik's and the fear he finds in them cleaves his heart in two. One after another, they disappear into the light.

Logically, he knows he should have paused, considered if jumping out of a moving train was the smartest move, if there was something else he could have done to help them, but love knows no reason, no logic to keep it grounded. He does not think, barely notes the distance between train and speeding grass, simply jumps toward the two boys he cannot live—or feel alive—without.

An Interlude

2023

*I*nez comes home to absolute darkness. A black so pure, so cloying, it is impossible to know where it ends and she begins. In the dark, she smiles. This will work, *she thinks*. It has to. *She flips the light switch to her left and shakes off the snow from her hair and coat before walking toward her two windows to inspect her work. Slowly, her fingers trace along the seams of the thick curtain, the nails she has hammered into the wall, making sure every edge lies flat.*

For hours that night, she avoids the inevitable. She reads every note and entry she's made in her little black notebook. She buries herself in research articles, scouring each one for something she may have missed, a source she's overlooked. Anything. But Inez knows that she's gleaned all she will from the scattered pages on her desk.

Her phone sits at its edge, and she unlocks it before changing her mind and quickly throwing it on the couch. Years, she's kept all of this to herself, held it so close to her chest that it became a part of her, and now, now that she is at the end of it all, she has the overwhelming urge to finally share it with her sister. She's kept this from her to keep her safe, has consciously chosen to not involve Mae in the mess she's made of her life, back when she didn't know Dev and Ravi like she does now. But Inez doesn't know how any of this will play out, and so she wants her to know, just in case.

She picks up her phone and sets it back down three times before finally tapping her contact photo. The phone rings twice, then goes to voicemail. She tries again, hoping it's the signal, and this time, Mae's phone rings for what feels like entire minutes before, again, going to voicemail.

"Hey, Mae, call me back. I need to show you something. Or tell you. I—I don't know," Inez says in one big breath. "I've wanted to tell you for a while, but I didn't know how. I think I do now. Just—just call me back." She hangs up and texts, in case Mae doesn't listen to her voicemail in time, and shoves the phone in her back pocket. She looks around her apartment, restless. She has wanted this for so long, and now there is nothing in her way. It is an exhilarating feeling, to reach the end of something. Which is why she finds it all too easy to ignore the voice in her head that says *wait*. Every second she stands here feels painfully, achingly, impossibly slow.

Inez roots around her desk looking for the notebook until she finds it again. She makes her way to the edge of the bed and pulls back the corner of the rug. Her fingernails find the wooden seams quickly, and she nudges the piece of hardwood open. She hides the notebook inside and returns the piece of wood where it belongs. Once she smooths out the carpet, it's like it was never there to begin with. The articles on the desk, the research, they *don't matter. Not in the way this notebook does, detailing every desperate thought she's had since she began this search four years prior, when she first heard rumors of the painting, back when it was just a myth. No. This is hers and hers alone. She finds it difficult to think of a time when she wasn't wholly consumed by it.*

Inez gets up, turns off the lights, and the apartment is suddenly a black hole. No light can escape. Nothing will make it in. She blindly feels her way around until her hands land on the closet doors. In the dark, she opens them, steps inside, and closes the doors behind her.

She sits down across from a painting, the *painting, and, even in the dark, can feel the magnitude of it. She runs her hands along its smooth and weaving surface, its chipped and fraying frame. For years she had imagined this moment, and so she takes a second to take it in, lets it wash over her in one overwhelming wave. It looms over her, but she sits there, steady and relentless.*

She does not waver.

Chapter 18
SEPTEMBER 10, 1891 12:03 A.M.

T he train roars past them as Ravi, Dev, and Nik lie in a heap on the ground.

Dev groans as he sits up. In the dim moonlight, he can see the fabric near his left knee is dark and damp. He touches it and winces. He's afraid to roll up the fabric, to see just how deep the cut is. For now, he wipes his bloody fingers against his sweater and stands, limping toward the others.

He spots Nik's small bound sketchbook and wallet a few feet away and groans as he picks them up. They must have tumbled out of Nik's pocket during the fall.

"Everyone all right?" he asks.

Ravi nods as he stands. Blood from a cut near his eyebrow drips down his temple, but he is otherwise unscathed.

"Nik?"

Nik still sits on the ground, his back to them. Dev takes a few strained steps toward him. It is difficult to ignore the sudden dread that builds in his stomach, that tells him something is very wrong. It isn't until he places a gentle hand on Nik's shoulder, twisting him toward him, that he sees the panic on his face.

Nik can't breathe.

He is gasping for air, forcefully pulling it into his lungs, but his breaths are shallow and his hand is at his chest, grasping for his heart, his throat. Nik looks up to see Dev, and the panic in his eyes mirrors his own. In a second, Dev is at his side. He falls to his knees on wet earth, and his hands go to touch Nik, to ease his pain, but there is nothing he can do. Nothing he can fix or give. He takes the panic that pours out of Nik, but it seems to be an endless stream, and in moments, they're both frantic.

"Ravi. Ravi, what do we do?" he asks, pushing Nik's hair out of his eyes, searching them with desperation for an answer, but Ravi is silent, frozen in place.

A few seconds later, Nik's breathing slows and the panic in them is quelled.

"Are you okay?" Dev asks, and Nik nods, though he looks pale beneath the full moon. "What was that?"

Before Nik can answer, Ravi finally speaks. "He's fine. Let's go."

"What?" Dev asks, incredulous. He turns toward his brother. "Did we both see the same thing?"

"Nik. You're fine. Right?" Ravi asks him, and Dev cannot comprehend his brother's reaction.

"Ravi, it's all right. You don't have to do that," Nik says, and his voice is so soft, so quiet, Dev has to strain to hear him.

"Someone explain to me what is happening right now."

Nik and Ravi share a long look, and again, Dev feels like he is on the outskirts of something, a wall too high to see past. Finally, Nik turns to Dev.

"My heart. It's no good," he says with a shrug, and Dev can feel the way each word chips at his own heart.

"What?" he asks, but it sounds like an answer. His knee throbs painfully, as if in response, and he falls back, collapsing onto the ground. His eyes don't leave Nik's.

"My parents are sending me away, to somewhere I can be treated properly, where I can get better." And at this part, his eyebrows go up, just the tiniest bit, but it's his tell, it always has been. Ever since they were children, every time Nik would tell the smallest lie, his eyebrows would race ahead of it. With it, any hope Dev had that this was something Nik could recover from, that there was a solution, dissipates. Suddenly, he understands.

He is going to lose him.

"When?" His voice is quiet, more measured than he feels.

"A week from now." Dev doesn't know what to say. Even though Nik sits inches from him, his green eyes locked on his, he feels only loss. He wants to scream, wants to turn to his brother and shove him to the ground for keeping this from him. But it wouldn't change anything. Suddenly, he is exhausted to the bone with helplessness.

He forgets they have left almost everything on a train already miles away, that all that's left is Nik's sketchbook and wallet, still clutched in Dev's hands. Forgets that they are stranded. For one fleeting moment, there is only Nik's dying heart and the loud thudding of his own in the stillness of the night. Then he thinks of his mother, bedridden, her mind trapped in a body that no longer belongs to her. It feels as if everything is slipping through his grasp, no matter how tight his fist.

Ravi clears his throat.

"We need a plan," he says gently. Neither says anything, both still look at each other in silence, and so Ravi offers a solution.

"The train hadn't stopped in a while; we can't be that far from the next town."

Like puppets they get up and walk, numb to the cold, to the ache, to even their destination. Dev does not care if they stay, if they go, and where; it's meaningless; hasn't the world already ended?

Ravi would have been the first to admit he didn't believe in any of this, that Dev had imagined, misremembered, what he had seen that night in the woods.

But there is no denying the force that had dragged him away from the train cabin and onto the ground. There is no denying the icy chill of the shadows as they wrapped around him before quickly dissolving into the dark. There is no denying that there is something at the end of this journey.

He looks back at Dev and Nik, who walk separately behind him. The distance between the two is a chasm. Should he have told Dev? he wonders—should he have broken Nik's trust months ago? Would that have made a difference? He does not know.

He thinks back to a moment ago when he stood there, use-less, as he watched Nik fight for breath. He knew it was foolish to deny what was happening in front of them, but he was des-perate to give Nik more time, to make up for the fact that when he thought he might lose him forever, all he did was stand there, still as the trees around him.

It's hours until they hear a sound. The building chatter of a bar, the settling sounds of a home. It's late, but there is life to be found everywhere. They approach the town sign that says PEMELTON, HOME OF THE HALIBUT, and all stop for a moment to stare at it.

"We're not even near a coast," Nik says, confused.

Ravi walks away and the two follow him. He stops near two horses tied to a stand, their backs heavy with bags from own-ers busy in the bustling bar a few feet away.

Ravi carefully approaches a horse. She's golden brown, her hair a bright white. Even in the dim light, her mane shines.

"Look at that palomino coat," he whispers, smiling. "A rare beauty." He reaches his hand forward and rests it on her side, slowly trails it up to her head until the two are looking at each other. At first the boys are confused as they watch Ravi slowly untie the horse from her wooden post. Ravi puts a finger to his lips to quiet them, and then motions for them to do the same to the gray horse a few feet away. *This is our ticket to Chicago*, he seems to say.

Dev begins to undo the knot as Nik greets her. Dev can't help but smile as he listens to Nik.

"I'm Nik, this is Dev. What's your name?" The horse, of

course, doesn't answer, but Nik takes the soft neigh as response enough.

"That's a beautiful name," he tells her as he runs his hands through her black-and-white mane. Dev wants to enjoy this simple moment for what it is, but his smile feels too heavy to hold. He lets it fall and focuses on the knot in his hands.

Quietly, the boys unclasp the bags resting on the horses' backs. They set them on the ground, and before the horses even know what's happening, Ravi is atop the brown one. Nik helps Dev onto the gray horse. His left leg still throbs, the fabric of his trousers stiff from the dried blood. He puts an arm around Nik's shoulder, and for a moment they pause, their faces so close they could kiss. It's Dev who looks away. Dev who finds it too painful to look at Nik knowing what he knows now. He pulls up onto the horse and makes room for Nik to do the same behind him. He jumps on and sits close behind Dev. Nik pretends not to notice Dev flinch when he tenderly places his hands on his waist. Neither says anything; every word between them feels too heavy and insufficient, and slowly they follow Ravi's horse away from the bar and through town, along the train tracks and on to Chicago.

The night is long, and Dev finds it too difficult to speak to Nik, as if it would make losing him later too painful to manage, never mind that he's spoken to him all his life, that he's known all of him so completely, unknowing him now would be an impossible feat. But here he is stubbornly refusing to answer Nik's questions with more than a word, his waist tensing at the touch of Nik's arms. Death is inevitable enough; why are some forced to become intimate with its intricacies, to know it so well for so long before they are allowed to embrace it? Why does his mother's body have to meet death sooner than her mind ever will? Why does Nik's heart have to fail him before he's even lived half a life? Dev doesn't have these answers. He only knows that the questions feel so heavy inside him, they could bury him.

Finally, just before dawn, they reach the edge of Chicago. The light softly whispers through the edge of the horizon, and they dismount once they reach a bar. There's a quiet bustling inside, glass against a wooden table, a soft conversation heard from outside.

"Do we have a plan?" Dev asks.

Ravi jumps off his horse. "To get a drink. We made it, didn't we?"

The boys get off their horse and tie her to the wooden post next to Ravi's. Dev notices Nik is in no rush to catch up to Ravi as the two keep a slow pace in silence a few feet behind him.

"I burned the book," Nik says.

"What?"

"The sketchbook. *I* burned it. My parents wanted to send me away months ago. And I just wasn't ready to leave . . ."

The sentence stops there, but Dev imagines Nik would have ended it with *you*.

And then he does.

"They let me stay if I promised to burn it. If I promised to put aside my silly love for art and botany. And as difficult as it was to follow through with it, it was an easy choice. Because it meant one last summer with you."

Dev stops in his tracks, stunned into stillness. He is convinced that Nik can hear the thudding of his heart, the echo in his rib cage. Years spent wondering, hoping, and now, finally, an answer.

"Why didn't you just tell me?" His voice breaks as he asks, but he doesn't try to hide his hurt. "If I had known the truth, I would have—"

"Would have what?" Nik interrupts. He stops in front of the bar, turning to Dev. Ravi has already disappeared inside. "There's nothing you could have done but look at me with pity."

He looks at Dev with such defiance, such openness, such fear, that Dev crumbles. For a quick second, Dev reaches forward and holds Nik's hand. One squeeze, a brush of a thumb against a wrist, and he lets go.

"I could have not wasted so much time," Dev says softly, and it's as if he's broken a piece of himself and given it to Nik.

Nik is standing so close to him that it feels impossible to look at anything but Dev's deep brown eyes. His full lips. His thick brows and their somber arch. Nik could hesitate, could second-guess this choice, could linger on this moment for so long, it passes. But Nik, who has always been convinced that he is only capable of loving Dev more than he has any right to, is tired of watching life go by. He leans forward and his parted lips meet Dev's. A part of him expects Dev to freeze, to pull away, but there is no hesitation on Dev's mouth. Only urgency. Inside Nik, entire gardens bloom and burn. He is forest and

Dev is fire. Nik feels the heat of him everywhere Dev's body brushes his. Dev's hands go to Nik's waist, and they grasp fistfuls of fabric. Nik stumbles back and finds himself pressed against the door of the bar. He loses his hands in Dev's dark hair. A thumb against a jaw, a hand against a neck. They are a collection of body parts strung together by want. By the time they part, they are breathless. They look at each other, chests heaving, lips swollen.

"There's hope still, Dev. If we find this painting," Nik says, breathless. There is a charcoal smudge on Dev's jaw from Nik's thumb. Nik smiles wide and wipes it off him, slowly, tenderly, before walking through the double doors and leaving Dev and his warm cheeks all alone beneath the purple-tinged morning sky.

Dev still reels as he follows him into the nearly empty bar. A bartender wipes the bar top as two men sit together at a table at the corner. Another sits by himself near the window nursing the last dregs of a glass of bourbon. Ravi sits at the counter, nursing a drink of his own. Dev can't read the small smile on his face, but blushes anyway. Neither mentions it.

"What can I get you boys?" the bartender says as Nik and Dev join Ravi.

"Information, actually," Nik tells him. And then Dev limps up to the counter. He does his best to ignore the pain shooting up his leg.

"Do you know where we can find Delphine Lefroy?" He clears his throat, finding his voice rougher than he expected.

The bartender shakes his head, but before he can answer, a voice near the window speaks up.

"Who's asking?" the man says. He raises the glass to his lips, lingering on the final sip, before setting it down on the table.

The boys look at one another, wondering who the man is. His long brown coat is worn and frayed at the collar. The edges of black trousers brush the tops of mud-caked boots, which rest on the chair opposite him, one leg crossed over the other.

He pauses to look at each of them. Dev straightens his back under his gaze. He is so close, he can taste this, just the edge of it. The boys have come all this way for Delphine Lefroy's painting. They aren't leaving without it.

"We're fans of her work, is all," Dev says, taking a gamble.

"I'm happy to tell you where her studio is. Once I've gotten another drink. But looks like my pockets are empty," he says, patting them.

Ravi rolls his eyes, and Nik puts down a few bills on the table.

"I'm awful thirsty, boys," the man says, and Nik puts down another note. Nik stands firm next to him, and the man takes the sketchbook from his hand and turns through the pages. Dev spots his own face again and again, a study of his hands, the back of his head with his hair in the wind. He notes all the moments Nik has been quietly watching, and his heart softens with each page. He looks up to find Nik's eyes already on him. *Here is my heart bare*, he seems to say. *Take it. It is yours already.*

The man recognizes Dev's face in the pages and looks up at them, an eyebrow raised. When he reaches an empty page, he quickly scrawls a map directing them to where Delphine Lefroy would be.

"If you're in search of the artist, you're a few weeks too late. She's long gone," he says as he hands back the sketchbook to Nik.

But it's not Delphine they need, it's what she's left behind. And so as the sun rises over the city and its people begin to stir, the three follow the map all the way to the X.

An Interlude

2024

*I*n the back seat of a black SUV sits a large painting made up of a white canvas. It sits quietly in the dark until Mae pulls open the driver's door and sits down. She clicks the overhead light on, and a warm glow fills the car. Mae doesn't glance over her shoulder. She is too focused on the small black cloth notebook in her lap. She leans back, resting her head against the window glass, and makes herself comfortable in the leather seat. She flips through the notebook quickly. Scribbles fill the lines, and she struggles to make out the words as they become more and more frantic, less and less coherent.

Finally, Mae looks over her shoulder to study the painting. Her eyes go immediately to the peeling edge, and she reaches out to touch it. She doesn't pull it, only feels it between her fingertips for two brief seconds before pulling her hand away.

A minute later she finds what she's looking for and runs out of the car, door ajar and notebook in hand. The painting is alone once again.

Chapter 19

Mae reads while Dev drives in silence. The overhead light shines on Inez's notebook as she takes in as much as her sleep-addled mind will allow, but the words are swimming on the page now. Inez's entries jump from the painting's history to tales that mention a woman made of shadows, clearly the same one from Dev's past. Pages about want and desire. Lists of Faustian tales she may have appeared in under different names, guises, benefactors begin to make sense. Moments when characters call out to the night and the night answers. She notes the differences in the stories. The one thing they all have in common? *The answer lies in darkness*, Inez underlined.

As Mae flips through the pages, she finds the same words scribbled in the margins again and again. Inez's apartment flashes through her mind, the way she had nailed the curtains to the wall. The room would have been pitch-black without the lights turned on. Mae doesn't know if it's anything, but it feels like the edge of a clue.

"I don't think we're supposed to have that on," he finally says, nodding toward the light.

"That's actually a myth. It's legal in most states, probably this one."

"Do you even know what state we're in?"

She doesn't miss his small smile that breaks through.

"Hence the probably."

They're quiet for a moment as Dev anxiously taps his fingers on the steering wheel. His scruff looks prominent under the harsh lighting above them, his eyes darker.

Mae cuts the silence. "Are you nervous about going back home?" She closes the notebook in her lap.

He finally notices his tapping fingers and stops. "I don't think it was ever truly home."

"What was?" she says, turning to him.

"I move around so much. I don't think I've ever had one." He meets her eyes for a second. "I spent time in Granada, in Spain, that felt as right as home could get."

"Why'd you leave?"

"I age. In both directions. People get suspicious over time. I can never stay in one place for too long, can never know the same people for too long. Home is hard when you run from it the second it catches up with you." He pauses for a long second. "I haven't gone back to where I grew up since I left, over a century spent avoiding it."

"What if it's gone? Couldn't you be wrong, and it was demolished years ago and we lost any trace of Ravi miles ago?" Even saying the words aloud fills her with panic, but it is a possibility impossible to ignore.

"It's there. I've kept tabs on it, to see if it's fallen to time and decay, but someone always buys it. Who knows. It could be Ravi, buying it with every new identity. He could never turn his back on the past, could never leave it behind or see it for what it was. Rowan Manor would always mean more to him than it should." He glances at his side mirror and switches lanes. He takes an exit that turns into a quiet side road, and eventually slows down, the gravel crunching beneath the tires.

Dev and Mae drive down the quiet tree-lined path and stop at the rusted gates. Here it lies, the gates of Rowan Manor towering over them both. They are overwhelming and intricate, and they are wide open, waiting for them. The two take a moment to look at each other, one last glance before driving into the great unknown. Dev is scared, she can see it in his eyes. She places her hand over his where it sits on the gearshift and stares straight ahead. There is a fleeting moment where he brushes his thumb against her pinkie. She feels the heat of it instantly and it warms her. She wants so badly to interlock her fingers with his, but the moment passes and Dev's hands are back on the wheel.

He drives a few feet farther, and finally, they see her car. Inside Mae, relief and dread swim together, settling in the pit of her stomach.

He parks at the edge of the gravel road and shuts off the Jeep.

"I don't know what he's planning," he says, turning to her. His eyes are unwavering. "But I need to know you're safe. Would you stay here, wait for me, if I asked?"

For a moment she considers it, but she can't come this close only for someone else to find her answers. Ravi knows what happened to her sister, may even have her now. She can't not go in. Mae has to find out what happened for herself.

She shakes her head and he understands.

"I figured," he says, nodding. He rubs the edge of the metal rabbit ear at the cane handle. He doesn't look at her. Only takes a moment or two before opening his door. "Then let's get this over with."

"Do we have a plan?" she asks.

"Do we ever?" They smile at each other and climb out of the car, road weary but with limbs buzzing for movement, for confrontation, for the same desire: to see this end. As they make their way down the gravel path, Mae takes a moment to look inside the back windows of her car, but the painting is gone. She catches up to Dev a few feet away and stops, looking up.

The house is massive, looming and decaying, its paint long since peeled. Vines climb the left side of the house, and in the dark, they look menacing, swallowing the home whole. At the right of the grand mahogany double doors stands a wide turret with windows rounding every exposed corner. Mae can see how it once could have been something to behold. She can imagine the light shining through unbroken windows, a garden tended to and cared for. A door open and welcoming.

But Dev doesn't see any of this. He only looks straight ahead, past the house and everything it holds, and starts toward the back. In the distance there is a cottage, its roof caved in, the door long gone. Mae watches as Dev averts his gaze, suppresses whatever memories it stirs, the ache.

He turns instead to a glass house before them, beautiful and wild in its abandon. A soft golden light emanates from the center of the greenhouse. Mae and Dev exchange a glance. There is not a doubt for either of them that Ravi, the painting, their answers, are waiting in the distance.

Beside her, Dev walks in silence, his eyes trained on the beacon that is the greenhouse. She reaches forward and squeezes his hand. In the dim light, with his brow furrowed, his eyes now on hers, she can't help but notice the way her heart lifts.

Mae pulls him closer and, before thinking twice, kisses him. An act of courage from her or for him, she doesn't know.

She can taste the shock on his tongue, in the way he's slow to react, his body frozen for a second too long. It is one brief moment that makes her doubt if she should have been as bold as she feels or if she should have swallowed it and marched forward toward the glow of the greenhouse. But soon enough he melts into her lips. She wonders if this is how sea feels against shore, made alive in its embrace, awoken as it crashes onto land. His arms wind around her waist as a hand snakes up her back and comes to rest along her jaw. He caresses the edge of her throat, and with every stroke, her pulse thuds faster.

If someone had found themselves along a path that led to Rowan Manor, they would have seen two figures in an embrace, silhouetted by the lamplight, like fire as it singed their edges.

If Dev and Mae had broken their embrace, they would have seen a figure silhouetted by the flickering flame of the glass house in the distance. His shoulders tight, the outline of his buzzed head crisp against the glow. But Ravi steps away before either of them notices and disappears amid the foliage barely confined behind the glass.

A small smile plays on Dev's lips and Mae grins back.

"I think I've been wanting to do that for two days," she says.

His smile falters, just for a second, and he pulls her close before she can wonder for too long. He takes a deep breath, his chest expanding around her, and steps away. There is no avoiding it now.

The greenhouse looms over them as they stand at its mouth. The door is wide open and wild greenery frames its edges, crawling out from where it is hardly contained. There is no method to its madness, no reason. The plants have overtaken this glass house from the inside out. The light filtering through is muted, smothered between the leaves. It dances in the warm breeze that curves and curls its way through the broken glass. Behind it, the sun is just beginning to rise.

Dev treads forward, pausing to hold an overgrown plant back for Mae. Finally, they step inside and let the wilderness swallow them whole.

Chapter 20

I n front of them stands the door to Delphine Lefroy's studio.

"What next?" Dev asks, and all three stare at it, wondering what to do now that they've come so close.

"Should we knock?" Nik asks.

"If she's gone, we might as well make ourselves at home," Ravi says. "Now, the matter of getting in . . . ," he mumbles to himself.

He turns around and scans the quiet street, looking for something. It is early in the morning, the sun only now beginning to rise, and he looks at the few passersby, choosing between them. Finally, a woman in a long sage-green dress with a cinched waist, flowing skirt, and pinned-up hair catches his eye, and he walks over to her, a soft smile playing on his lips.

Dev and Nik watch as he stops the woman. They are too far to hear what he is saying to her, but she looks startled at first until she laughs at something he says. After a few seconds, her hands go to her hair and she takes out a hairpin keeping a curl in place. A lock falls over her shoulder, and when Ravi speaks again, the boys can see the woman blush all the way from where they are standing. Ravi jogs back to them as the woman looks over her shoulder wistfully at him and continues on her way, with one less hairpin than before.

He holds it up to them with a smile, all teeth and boyish charm, and bends down to better pick the lock with the hairpin. His hand tests the brass handle, expecting to find it firm and immovable. He expects to have to pick at the lock until he feels the gears falling into perfectly synchronized place, but instead, Ravi twists the handle, and the door yawns open to them.

Ravi and Nik share a look of unease. They wonder if perhaps this has been too easy, if they are walking into a trap. They are, after all, seeking the impossible. Shouldn't it be more difficult? Shouldn't the door at least be locked if it hides what they want most in this world?

Dev knows better. He has been warned after all.

They step inside to find a modest studio, dusty and untouched. Light filters through large curved windows. The curtains are spread wide open and the windows are shut. It is bright and wide and airy and beautiful, and yet, the space isn't warm. It's cold and unwelcoming in a way none of the boys can understand. But the cold is inconsequential next to the focal point of the room.

A white painting stands at its center.

On an easel is a large canvas surrounded by an ornate golden frame, newly polished and shining in the early morning light. Dev steps closer and studies the clean white brushstrokes, the curling corner on the top left-hand side. His thumb rests on the gold-plated edge as he follows the dips and slopes of the frame.

Dev has no doubt this is it. This is what they've come all this way for.

"It's about time, my dear boys," a voice says, and they all turn to look for the source. But they might as well have heard it inside their heads, this bodiless voice as loud as their thoughts. A moment later, a woman appears in the corner of the room, and though all could swear she wasn't there before, all would doubt their own version of the truth. Had she been there all along? Had all three missed her entirely? For one quick moment, out of the corners of their eyes, Ravi and Nik wonder if it's Delphine Lefroy sitting in the shadows, her legs draped over the velvet chair.

But no.

In the light, Dev can finally see her clearly. The woods, the train, he was close, but it was always too dark, too quick. Now, in the bright morning light of the studio, he can watch as the shadows drift over her, around her. She leans her head back and the dark follows. Her shoulder peeks through, the dip of a collarbone, but no matter how she moves, the shadows move with her. When she turns, the white cloud that is her hair peeks through, and then, just as suddenly, the gloom wraps its way around once again.

If he were to look closer at the room instead of the woman, he would notice she needs to take to be here. Needs to pull the shadows from the rest of the space to exist in it. He does not see the room for what it is: the wilted flowers with no silhouette, the too-bright hardwood beneath the easel, the shadowless corners. All of it wrong, unnatural. But he doesn't notice any of it.

He only sees her.

"I see there is something each of you want," she says, her eyes cold, impassive. "Something you have come all this way for, hoping that I would be kind enough to grant it, that this painting held enough magic for each of you to share." She shakes her head, smiles, but it is full of menace. Of anger and scorn and bitterness all rolled into one. "As if it belonged to you. As if you are all deserving, to have your benign, mundane wants made into reality."

She stands and walks across the room, lingering at the painting for a moment. Her hands trail along the top of the frame, a quick stroke of her thumb against the peeling edge. She takes her time as the boys watch. Logic fights against what they see, this almost shape-shifting woman made of night, but who could deny her? Her movements feel like water, like light. Or more accurately, like shadows slipping through cracks. It dawns on two of them how completely they've misunderstood the rules of the game, how this will not be as simple as asking. Dev, though, knew better. She drifts across the room like a setting sun until she makes her way to the first of the weary travelers.

"Niklaus Rowan." She savors the complexity of the sound, crisp, then round, then smooth. "A boy with a weak heart who wishes for health. But it's not a new heart you truly seek. You ask for health, but what you mean is freedom. The freedom needed to never rely on family money, on their status. A healthy heart will mean you will never have your hand forced to do their bidding in order to simply survive. You seek to leave the stifling confines of the home your family so painstakingly built," she says, pouting her lips. "If it was up to you, you would never see your family again." She holds Nik's chin, but there is nowhere else for his focus to be. "You, Niklaus Rowan, seek to disappear."

She circles the three boys, touches the back of Nik's neck with a tip of a nail, an edge of a shadow. He shivers at the touch but doesn't move away.

"Ravi Sharma." She laughs like bells chiming out of key, teasing. Laughing *at* him. "You believe you want money, the means to begin again, never to be trapped beneath Niklaus's thumb, his favor. To never let your father look down on you again for *needing*. To step away from Dev's shadow and be your own man." She puffs out her chest as she says this, the shadows fanning out around her, allowing her to take up more space. "To never be ruled by anyone else again. It is not money that grants you this. It's power."

The others look at him. Dev is so rarely surprised by his own brother. It's Ravi he knows better than anyone. Better than himself some days. But Ravi doesn't deny it. All three know it as fact. Know that for every word the woman utters, she can only speak truth. Without knowing how or why, they know her tongue has never tasted a lie. Ravi doesn't look at either of them, only keeps his eyes locked on the woman inches from him. She bares her teeth in a sneer and steps away.

She mocks them, says their wants out loud for the others to hear. And of course she saves Dev for last. She grins, her eyes wide and bright.

"And you, Dev." Her voice is a snake, its tongue brushing down the back of his neck. "You want it all."

He interrupts her before she can continue, shaking his head in defiance, stubbornness. "I know what I want."

Her eyes widen, amused. "Oh?"

"I want Nik and my mom to be okay. I don't want them to suffer, I don't want them held captive in bodies that continue to betray them every day. I just—I just want them to be okay."

She laughs. A genuine laugh that erupts from her belly. It echoes in the quiet of the room. "That is not what you want most, my dear boy."

His eyes catch Nik's. He watches as Nik takes a deep breath, a sigh really, and smiles. It's a sad smile though, and it tears at Dev's heart. Because he knows, Dev realizes—Nik knows him. In one heavy smile, Nik forgives him—for being selfish, for being scared. Dev sees this clear as day and cannot bear it, cannot bear this feeling in his chest, and looks away.

He turns to the woman with no name.

"Maybe not, but it's what I choose all the same," Dev says.

She shakes her head. "I only trade in deepest desires, and those are never a choice, my boy. They are a need." Her eyes are wicked, cruel, as they greedily drink the shame that the truth brings these boys.

She steps back, extending arm and shadow, and addresses all of them. "Dev wants more than any of you. Which means he will give more than any of you to get it." Her eyes land on his. "Won't you, Dev?" she asks, though it isn't a question. He can deny it, of course, but all three know it to be true. She will not lie, after all.

"But just how much are you willing to give for eternal life and everlasting youth? To escape dying altogether?"

She says the words aloud, and it's as if she has unraveled him. There is no use lying. No use trying to convince her that what he wants most is to deny what he wants most. She knows what he cannot bear to say. And despite how it tears at his soul, he knows there is nothing to do but accept his own truth.

"*That's* what you want?" Ravi spits.

Dev realizes neither of them knew the other all that well.

"Anything," he says quietly, but his whisper fills the silence more than his brother's shout. Dev looks straight ahead, avoiding the stares from Nik and Ravi. He cannot see how they look at him, did not come all this way to turn back now.

The woman is terrifying in her satisfaction, in the destructive wake of the truth. "The deal is simple. A life for a life."

Three pairs of eyes face her, all wide and questioning.

"Do I shock you?" she says, laughing. "The balance of things must always be restored, Dev. Sacrifice others to the painting and your own life is reset. You will age again, and you will sacrifice again. But your body will live in this moment, forever connected. Along with your weaker half," she adds, and there is a cruel sort of smile that slashes across her face.

"Me? I don't want this. I don't want any of it." Ravi looks at his brother, waits for him to protest, and is stunned to see his brother stand there, silent.

She shrugs. "You're his twin, are you not? Entered this world together, bound by blood and fate. Let this be one more thing that binds you to him. It feels apt, don't you think?"

"No, it doesn't," he pleads. "Not when the choice has been taken from me. Not when someone else must die for him to have this."

She tilts her head, studying him. "And aren't you curious to see how far your brother is willing to go to have this? Do you expect me to give Dev everything he desires without expecting him to give away what matters most?"

"You said a life for a life," Dev says, his voice low, measured. "Which life?" He never thought he could be capable of such monstrous things. And yet, he stands here still, considering.

"Dev," Ravi shouts, and the word drips with disgust. "Stop. This is no way to live a life, cursed to never move forward all because you're too afraid of what will come. Don't do this. Please."

Dev doesn't respond, only looks at the woman as she walks around them, wraps a shadowed arm around Nik's shoulder before it trails away.

"You'll have to sacrifice Niklaus to the painting. To peel that curling corner back and let him be consumed by it. The first of many. But the first he must be." She whispers this last part in Dev's ear, but it's as if she's whispered it to all of them.

"Not Nik, no," Dev says, and this response is immediate and full of horror.

She shakes her head, smiles. "This is what immortality will cost. I have no use for these souls myself, only hunger for particular ones, but nevertheless. There are consequences for this sort of magic. Sacrifices need to be given, payments made."

"Then choose something else, anyone else," he says, standing firm. He can't give Nik. He won't. Nik with all his love and kindness and vastness. How can he take that for himself? How can he live with himself if he does?

For a moment, the smile slips from her sharp face. "I will not make this easy for you, Dev. You want this? Show me."

He glances at Nik, who watches them both. He does not fight, does not curse at him or walk away. He watches and he waits. This boy with his dying heart, who was going to leave him in a week's time anyway.

The woman walks around to the back of the easel and rests her hands on the gold frame. "Will you accept this gift of eternal life if it means your brother is cursed to live forever? If it means the only boy you've ever loved is sacrificed to the very magic that will keep you alive?"

Dev opens his mouth, but nothing comes out. Losing Nik would hurt. But it was always going to hurt, and he was always going to lose him.

Ravi speaks first. "Dev wouldn't do that. He wouldn't trade us for this ridiculous wish." Ravi begins to walk away, but he is the only one heading for the door.

Nik stays in place, eyes firmly on Dev. He knows Dev. He know the way his face falls when he talks about his mother, how he checks his hands for tremors when he thinks the others aren't looking, the first sign of her illness. And he knows the way Dev looked at him when he told him he was dying, a mix of love and fear. The fear would always win. He knows Dev is so acutely afraid of dying, he'd give anything to escape it altogether. Including Nik.

Ravi turns to Dev.

"You can't seriously be considering this."

Dev doesn't say anything.

"Don't pout, Ravi," the woman says with fake concern. "With time comes power. Patience you'll have to find for yourself. And Nik," she says, turning to him. "You'll disappear, never to see your family again. Just like you wanted."

Ravi ignores her. "Dev," he says as he walks toward him, his steps heavy and quick.

Nothing. He only stares at the floor, at their shoes, feet apart.

"This is Nik we're talking about. Nik. You love him. I know you do."

Dev looks up. His eyes meet Nik's over Ravi's shoulder, and he hates that all he finds there is forgiveness. Why can't he yell, fight? Why can't he tell Dev how horrible of a person he is? This acceptance makes him feel even sicker for what he is about to do.

"These are her rules. Her conditions. I didn't choose them," Dev says, his eyes back on Ravi, who is beyond incredulous.

"No, you can't turn this. *You're* choosing this. You're choosing to give Nik up to her. You're choosing to bind me to this, to you, when I'm telling you I don't want this. No part of me wants this. Death, dying, they are unfortunate parts of life. You cannot escape them."

"But now we can. Don't you see? They don't have to be

inevitable. Life can be ours for the taking, free from failing bodies and lives cut short. This is the way out." Dev wants this. He hates how much he does, but it doesn't change the facts. It roils in his belly, acidic and awful, and for a moment he wonders if he will have to carry this feeling with him forever. If what he wants to do is so reprehensible, he will never forgive himself for it as long as he inexcusably lives.

And it will be a very long time.

"At what cost," Ravi asks, but it isn't a question. They stare at each other in silence. Over Ravi's shoulder, Dev sees Nik looking at the painting, beginning to head for it.

Ravi follows Dev's eyes and sees it, almost in slow motion, as Nik, inches from the painting, reaches for the curling corner. Ravi twists, launching himself in Nik's direction in an attempt to stop him. For a single fleeting moment, Dev is frozen in place. He watches as his brother wraps his arms around Nik, trying to pull him back.

And then Dev's legs begin to move. He doesn't go to Nik, but past him, walks around the painting and stands behind it.

Later, he will try to remember this moment as if it was out of his control. As if Dev and his body were two and it was his body that led him here.

Mechanical.

Automatic.

Removed.

But that isn't true. Each step Dev makes is a choice. And when he reaches over the painting to pull the peeling edge for Nik, he cements all three to the fate the woman in the shadows has bestowed upon them. As he pulls it back, Nik elbows Ravi in the stomach, one hard and quick hit that has Ravi recoiling. He lets go of Nik and clutches his side.

It is all Nik needs.

Nik looks to Dev one final time and has the audacity to smile. An almost goodbye to the boy who's choosing life over love, immortality over him. *If I must die, why not for the boy I love?* he seems to say.

And then he's gone.

Chapter 21

At the far end of the room stands Ravi. His back is to them as he stares down at the painting he has laid against the table.

"Hello, brother," he says without turning around. He has been waiting for this for over a hundred years, and so he lingers, savoring the moment. All he has is time.

"I need to take it back. You know that."

Ravi turns to look at him in bewilderment. "You think this is yours to take?" One quick laugh escapes him. "It's over, Dev."

Dev doesn't say anything. Only glances at the painting that rests a few feet behind Ravi.

"Are you—" Ravi begins, finally turning to her.

She nods, wary and resolute all at once. "Mae. Her sister."

"I didn't know she had one," he says softly. A small smile pulls his mouth, and it is sadder than any smile ought to be.

"Where is Inez?" she asks forcefully, her hands fists at her sides. She is hopeful for answers, any answers. But he only ignores her question.

"What has he told you? About why you're here, about the painting, the part he plays in it."

"Dev's told me everything," she says, but Ravi's tone undoes the firmness with which she believes this.

"I highly doubt that." Ravi stands in front of the painting, blocking it from Dev's ravenous stare. "You wouldn't be here if he did."

"What is he talking about?" She looks at Dev, hoping to find assurance in his eyes, some confirmation that she shouldn't trust Ravi, but he glares at him, his jaw clenched, his eyes burning. He avoids her look. There is a sort of resolve in his stance, as if he's always known this moment would come, had resigned himself to its inevitably the moment he stepped inside the greenhouse. She wonders if his earlier plea for her to stay in the car was a final attempt at keeping the truth from her.

"He's talking about how I lied to you," he says, finally tearing his eyes away from Ravi to look at her. "About who made the deal and who was forced into it."

She takes a step back, as if her body craves to put distance between them. "That can't—you wouldn't ha—" She shakes her head, trying to understand. He doesn't say anything. Only looks back at her with what she thinks is remorse. She isn't sure, doesn't know who to trust anymore.

"You told her it was me?" Ravi says, laughing. "How noble of you. By all means, make me the villain. Tell her I forced your hand. That I was the one to give Nik away. That I spent a hundred years running."

"Nik?" Mae asks. She is reeling from how little she knows. How much she's misunderstood.

"Nik. The first of the sacrifices and the love of Dev's life." He lingers on every word. Looks at Dev as he says it.

"Ravi," Dev says, and it is a whisper, like the word scrapes against his throat on the way out. "Stop," he pleads. It's clear how this part of the story hurts, even after more than a century's worth of distance, why he kept it out of even his version of the lie. For a moment, there are no layers of Dev to peel back, no agenda, no mask to see through. It is Dev, and he is scared and vulnerable and begging for Ravi to stop talking.

"Did you care about Inez too? When you gave her the painting? When you forced her into it?" Ravi asks, and venom drips from his mouth.

"I didn't force her into anything, and I didn't make her pull it," Dev says defensively, but just as quickly, it turns into something else, an admission. "I knew she would eventually. I just didn't think it would all happen so quickly. Most people, it takes years as the corner slowly unfurls, as they grow more and more curious. I didn't need the time her sacrifice would grant me yet."

Mae is stunned into silence. How had she fallen for it so quickly, trusted Dev so completely?

"I don't—I don't believe you," Ravi says, shaking his head. "She knew. She knew about all of it. She wouldn't have pulled it back knowing what would happen. We'd made this plan together. Her moving in next door, befriending you, all of it." He walks toward Mae, desperate for someone to agree, to see what he sees. "Dev was looking to pass along the painting to someone new, all she had to do was make sure it was her. I knew of the dangers in our plan, and yet I was desperate enough to let her get closer than I had any chance of ever being. She was willing to get the painting back because she knew the truth of its history and loved me anyway, wanted to spend a lifetime together, grow old together. Which meant taking it from him and sacrificing no one to it." He turns to Dev again as denial rages through him. "You did this. I don't know how, but you forced her into sacrificing herself."

Dev shakes his head. "I'm sorry. She's in that painting, but I didn't put her there. Not directly anyway."

With those words, Mae realizes she was still holding on to the hope that Inez was out there, that there was a piece of the puzzle she hadn't yet found. But all Dev did was prey on that hope. Mae stares at the painting, looking for her sister in its canvas. How had she not realized? How had she not known she had been with Inez for days?

"How could you?" Mae asks, turning on him. "I trusted you. Believed you when you told me some sob story about being cursed. When all along Inez was in the car the entire time. Because you put her there?" She is incredulous, face flushed, voice rising with every word. She feels the anger collecting in her belly, can sense the way it builds within her.

"Please, Mae," Dev says, ready to crumple at her feet. "The past two days, I hated lying to you, hated knowing I hurt you. That's the truth." He looks at her with such earnestness, she almost breaks. She doesn't want to believe any of it, but everything begins to click. Inez's frantic research. Anthony, the missing owner. Even Dev's need to come along on this trip. It was to keep an eye on the painting, to not lose it to Mae. He made a new plan the moment they found the painting in the closet. He was buying time.

"I didn't mean for any of this to happen. I didn't know she had anyone. I wouldn't have given it to her if I had known. I'd spent so long being precise about my choices. The people I gave it to, they were cruel, or selfish. But occasionally"—he pauses here, forces the words out—"they were people that wouldn't be missed."

She glares at him and the fury she feels rips her open. She lunges for him, her hands closing into fists as she pummels his chest. Something guttural escapes her throat, but it doesn't surprise her. She is pain and grief and betrayal fused together. She is rage incarnate. He stumbles back and they plummet to the ground, the dead leaves and damp dirt muffling their fall.

For a few seconds, he doesn't fight back, doesn't defend himself or block her hits. He lets her screams turn to tears, lets her squeeze her wrath into a fist until he's bloody and bruised.

And then. A shift.

He grips her, his hands tight around her wrists, and pushes her away, as if he's paid his penance, as if this is punishment enough.

He stands, but Mae is too tired to follow. She stays on the ground, slumped and broken and empty. There is nothing left of her.

"Every time I turn a certain age, the tremors set in," he tells them both. "The age comes faster every time. And every time I'm desperate to beat the clock. To find someone before the rest of the symptoms set in. This began as an attempt to escape a possibility, now all I do is evade an inevitability. It's no excuse. I know. But she was there, and she was curious, and it was all too easy."

His face is cold, impassive. "I'm sorry you lost her to the painting," he says to Ravi. "But you shouldn't have involved her." He picks up his cane and straightens his shoulders. "I'll need it back now."

Remorseful Dev is gone, shelved and put away to make room for the Dev that will fight tooth and nail to get the painting back, to deny himself the future he refuses to face.

Ravi steps toward him, daring him to try. For a moment, the boys tower above her and Mae watches, as if in slow motion, as Dev grips the rabbit head in his fist and, with one swift arc, strikes his brother against the head, the raised scales of the steel snake digging into his tender skin.

Blood splatters against Mae's face, Inez's borrowed shirt.

Ravi stumbles, his back against the rough wooden table, and Dev goes after him, fists at the ready.

Watching Dev, it is clear to Mae that the painting is only a thing, that it stokes nothing but curiosity. Dev may have spent decades afraid of what would happen if he couldn't give it the one thing it needed, afraid of what came after, but he is its driving force. He is the demon he fears. For two days, he traded his demon for a hero and let someone else assume his mantle. For two days, he let Mae, himself, think he was worth saving.

And suddenly, Mae doesn't care about the details, about his weak justification, about the false guilt he's so quick to put aside. She tears her eyes away from their brawl. She wants nothing to do with either of them. What she does want is the last two days back, but without them, she wouldn't be here, in a greenhouse in Vermont with two brothers she's only just met who knew a part of Inez she'll never get to meet. They took that from her. And so, she makes a decision.

She'll take the painting for herself.

She crawls toward it, her knees damp from the wet ground. In time, she will unlock its mysteries, find a way to release her sister. The boys are too invested in their century-long feud to even notice that she's quietly dragging it along the dirt floor. Behind her, the brothers crash into the glass wall, landing on the other side of it.

This is her chance. But as Mae rushes to stand with the painting in her hands, her foot catches on a root and they both tumble forward with a thud, her face scraping against the detailed frame. Blood drips down her jaw as she tries to pick it up again. But she's panicked now. Her heart sprinting in her chest. Over her shoulder, she sees the boys rushing back at the sound of her fall. But she isn't looking when she goes to pick it up again, when her hand slips and catches the peeling edge instead.

Whispers encompass the three, as if desperate for air, for light, euphoric at the inch Mae has accidently granted them. Within them is Inez, clear as a bell.

Mae.

Her heart is in her throat. Here she is! Inez. She can hear her. So real and so alive. All she wants is to see her sister, to save her from wherever she is. Mae kneels down and reaches for the curling corner. She doesn't fully understand how it all works, just knows a thin layer of paint separates her and Inez, but a thought works its way through: Could she evade its magic? Could she pull it back and move out of the way in time?

Inches away from the painting, she sees the small sliver of paint beneath the peeling edge shifting. The glow of a flickering flame shifts and twists in subtle movements, more alive than it has any right to be. Her fingers make contact with the paint— softer than it should be, pliable still after so much time—and she hears the small gasp that escapes Ravi's mouth from over her shoulder. She isn't too fast for either of them to stop her, but they stand frozen in fear of the power this painting holds.

Mae tugs farther, and whispers fill the greenhouse. She can't make sense of them, can't decide if she really is picking out Inez's soft voice from the tangle anymore, but the voices feel so close, she could swear a century's worth of sacrifices surround her, flitting from one shoulder to the other.

"No," Dev cries above the whispers, but he's speaking to himself just as much as Mae. He stands behind her. He knows better than to look, and yet he can't pull his eyes away fast enough. Mae knows she should move, flee, create a distance from her and whatever took her sister, but she is in awe, taking it in.

Beneath the peeling white paint is a beautiful oil portrait of this moment. Soft brushstrokes show the orange glow of the oil lamp lighting the barely contained flora within the glass walls. Dev stands over Mae's shoulder, his face frozen in fear. The edges of him burn against the light.

Mae continues to tug at the painting to reveal her own eyes. Then, almost as if she's imagined it, the eyes change. They're Inez's eyes, she can swear it. For a moment she wonders if it's the lack of sleep, the heat, a hallucination, but the eyes that stare back say otherwise. After months of searching, of wondering and wanting and wishing and wavering, Inez is here. She is looking back with the same eyes Mae has known all her life. She goes to pull more, to see more of her long-lost sister, a nose, a mouth, the scar on her chin, but the paint pulls back. It doesn't let her tug any farther. There is only Dev and eyes that should be her own but aren't.

For Dev, it is too late. His own painting is too quick, too instinctual. It knows his every move. When he shifts to the left, the hands are already there to meet him. They grab hold of his shirt and pull. His once pained, painted expression is menacing now.

Ravi sees what's happening, and as much hate as he holds for his brother, he has just as much love. He had been prepared to kill Dev, to end both of their lives once and for all. But this? He had never wished this endless purgatory on his brother. Not once in a hundred and thirty-three years. He lunges forward and grabs ahold of his brother's hand. Dev looks back, fear clear as day behind his eyes as their fingers lock, but the painting, light and shadow morphed into a Dev that looks more like him than he does, is too strong, too powerful. Soon enough, his fingers slip away, and he is inside. There is only one Dev now.

They do not know for certain if the Dev they see is theirs or the imitation, but deep down, they understand it is somehow both. Mae hates how she wants to reach out and touch him, save him, pull him back into this world. Instead, she watches as the original peeled layer melts away and becomes part of the canvas once again, as his reversed hands disappear beneath the frame and come back with a brush, the white paint dripping from its bristles.

An Interlude

2024

*D*ev *is pulled in by his own portrait. It's his mirrored eyes that look back from the canvas, his reversed hands that rush forward past the frame and grasp his own shirt. He can feel the wetness of the oil paint when the angry painted boy's knuckles graze his collarbone. Here it is, a warped and crueler version of him who takes him deep inside. He wonders if it is a century's worth of his own sacrifices that are behind the vitriol he feels swimming around him. The chorus of voices hiss a single unanimous* yessss, *as if they can read his thoughts.*

He wonders if they are one voice short.

Soon enough, they are one, and Dev is staring back at Mae and Ravi with desperation in his eyes.

He feels he is sinking, only a shadow of himself now. From inside, he can see how his body moves without his consent. He sees how he bends at the waist to reach a pail of white paint, a wet paintbrush resting on top. He knows what he is being forced to do from the countless others who have been sacrificed before him. He is powerless as, slowly, his fingers wrap around the brush. He tries to fight against it, to loosen his grasp, stiffen an arm, but shadows have no bearing on reality. They are only imitations of what they stand against. Where it leads, they follow.

Dev straightens and begins to make large, sweeping strokes. The paint is thick and heavy as it drips from the paintbrush. Inez's eyes are the first to go. And the others watch as he seals his own tomb. Soon enough, the brushstrokes have covered everything he can see. All there is is piercing white and the devastating realization that Dev's eternal life will continue, just not how he had planned.

Chapter 22

The whispers flee the greenhouse, silenced by the final brushstroke, and it is just Ravi and Mae now. Ravi finds himself on his knees, staring at the painting. Mae watches as tears streak his cheeks. From relief or grief, she does not know, but she wonders if it is both. The canvas is already dry. The only proof of the minutes previous is a missing Dev. At the sound of a soft crackle, she sees the corner of the painting begin to curl outward.

"I'm taking it," she tells him.

"I can't let you do that." He doesn't look at her or stand as he says it, only seems to collapse deeper to the ground. There is no fight left in him. She sees that.

"Inez is inside there. If she was pulled in, she can be pulled out. I don't know how or when or where to even start, but I know that if there's a way, I'm going to find it. The painting stays with me." For the first time, Mae's voice doesn't waver or quake. There is no fear inside her to rattle her words. Ravi finally meets her eyes and sees in her what she knows to be true. She won't leave this greenhouse without Inez.

He looks at her with something like pity, as if she's naive to think it possible. But in the end he agrees. "It's yours and yours alone. If anyone is given to it, if it takes anyone at all, I will find you and I will destroy it. You will have left me no choice."

She nods. This will mean that Ravi does not get to die here and now. He doesn't get the absolution he's craved just yet. Instead, he will grow old. He will live one final swift life. He owes her this. Neither can deny it. But his terms are fair, and so she grabs the painting and heads out, ready to put this greenhouse behind her. She hears him blow out the fire in the oil lamp and stand. He catches up to her and they walk side by side back to the car. She notices he's taken Dev's cane with him. She hadn't realized Dev dropped it. He grips it at the center, his palm around the black metal of the winding snake.

It's morning now, a sliver of the moon still apparent but quickly fading. Mae cannot believe that forty-eight hours ago, she was home with no knowledge of what Inez was involved in. And now here she is holding her. Sort of. She should feel tired. Drained. And she does. But for the first time in two days, a cool, brisk breeze whips through her hair and she feels braver than she's ever been. Capable of anything. Like telling her parents she's taking a year off. Or finding a way out for Inez. Maybe the answers lie in Chicago. It's where this all truly began after all. Maybe it was always inevitable that she would make her way there.

He unlocks her car, and she tucks the painting in the back seat, back where it belongs. Gently, she shuts the door and takes the keys from Ravi. The moment they land in her palm, she breathes a sigh of relief so large, it holds an entire day inside it.

Her hands go to her pocket for Ravi's keys, but she realizes she doesn't have them. "Dev had your keys," she says simply.

He shrugs. "You don't live as long as I have and not know how to hot-wire a car."

They stand in silence for a moment. Unsure of where to go from here.

"You know, she had ended things right before when he must have gifted her the painting, right before she went missing," Ravi says. He seems compelled to bare his soul to Mae, an attempt to set down the weight he has been carrying. She lets him. "Said she was tired of being used, that she wanted nothing to do with our century-long feud. I couldn't blame her. It wasn't until the gallery owner called to say you were asking about her that I realized what had happened. By then I had noticed I was aging back, but I didn't know—I didn't think he'd—" He takes a deep breath. "I just wish I knew why she pulled it."

His words trigger something in Mae. "When I was at her apartment, I found her blackout curtains nailed to the wall. I keep thinking about a line she wrote in her notes. *The answer lies in darkness.* Do you know what she meant?"

He looks away. His brows knit together, and then his eyes widen in realization. "She wouldn't. Couldn't have," he mumbles. "Once, we'd talked about ways to call on the woman made of shadows, forcing her to take back this curse. In all my years, I'd never seen her again. Inez mentioned stories she'd read, where characters called on beings of power, reminiscent of the woman made of shadows. Inez wondered if deep desire, pure belief, a powerful object connected to the woman, and of course, darkness could lure her, could create a space for her to come. It was pure speculation. I didn't think she'd do it."

Mae can see his gears working, trying to place this new piece of the story with what he already knows. This piece that doesn't fit quite right. Had she done it for him, to save him? But by then, she'd ended things. Did she have her own plans all along? Her own reasons for calling on the woman with no name? She wonders if he's beginning to root through their memories, looking for signs he may have missed.

It dawns on her then. "The book, *The Picture of Dorian Gray*. It was you that wrote the note, wasn't it?"

He smiles, lost in the memory, and they're both quiet for a moment.

"I loved her, you know," Ravi says. "Two short years of this long life I could never forget." He pauses before continuing. "I'm sorry. She was only meant to be a messenger. I should have never involved her, and I'll regret that for the rest of my life." His voice breaks at the end, and he clears his throat and looks away. Mae's brow furrows, but only for a second. Just as quickly, she smiles and thanks him for the words, no matter how empty they feel.

She doesn't tell him the notebook dates back four years, that Inez may have known what she was getting into more than she let on. That maybe, just maybe, she was the one that sought him out, Dev, the painting. Her own answers. Instead of telling Ravi any of this, she lets him keep whatever innocent memories he has of Inez, no matter how muddled they may seem now. There is no use taking that away from him too.

In the quiet between them, Mae stares at Ravi and tries not to see Dev. But the similarities are so apparent, it pains her to look at him, to have him so close, this boy who took everything from her. She looks away, studies the keys in her hand for a moment, and when she looks up again, Ravi is gone. He walks to his truck, his face angled toward the sun the whole way there.

For a fleeting moment, she considers calling him back. He is after all the only person who might know more about the painting, who might be able to help. The only person who loves Inez almost as much as she does. But she decides against it. He's done enough. She won't grant him the absolution he craves by getting her out, no matter how skeptical he is of her chances. She has the painting, Inez's notes. She has time. She will do this on her own.

Inside, she starts the car and turns it around. Ravi drives ahead of her past the gate, and once they reach the road, he turns left. She inches forward and, a few seconds later, turns right, leaving Ravi in her rearview mirror.

Mae doesn't know where to go from here, how to go about saving Inez. All Mae knows is there are still questions she doesn't know what to do with. But she's closer than she was two days ago, and maybe that's enough for now.

An Interlude

The painting lies in the back seat of a car. The people inside it are shadows of what they once were, only now with one new addition. A girl takes the painting and drives all the way home. She carefully pulls it out of the back seat and places it in her room. Her parents come in, asking questions she does not answer. Not yet. She does not have the heart to give them hope only to rip it from their hands when nothing comes of it.

No.

She will wait.

Wait until she can back up the answers she has with tangible proof.

For years, she keeps it close. It follows her to Chicago where Mae continues her sister's research, diving into similar unexplainable objects, tales of a woman with snow-white hair and black eyes deep as coal who offered things beyond imagination. She'll spend a lifetime if she must, trying to release Inez and everyone else who has been trapped inside. Though if she can't free one boy in particular, maybe that would be okay. She tries not to stare at it too long but some nights she can't help it. She can feel him behind the thin layer of paint, knows that if she were to pull back the peeling edge, the frantic whispers would fill the room. For now, she keeps the painting near, comforted by the knowledge that if he's close, then so is Inez.

Acknowledgments

There's a monologue in *Fleabag* that Andrew Scott gives, the "Love Is Awful" speech, that breaks my heart every time. Often, it feels awfully applicable to writing. To paraphrase the Priest, "being a [writer] takes a hell of a lot of hope. I think what they mean is, when you find [an idea] that you love, it feels like hope." Publishing a second book is nothing like your debut. Ask anyone but the lucky few. Every word here, I pulled out of me like a splinter and then marveled at how there was nothing I'd rather be doing, even then. And so, when he says, "It's all any of us want, and it's hell when we get there. So no wonder it's something we don't want to do on our own," I think of everyone below and how this book wouldn't exist without them.

First and foremost, to everyone who read, posted, shared, borrowed, and bought *A Guide to the Dark*, I am eternally grateful. To Jess Harold and the entire team at Holt, I'm so lucky to have you all in my corner. This has been a dream come true, and that's because of each and every one of you. To Jennifer March Soloway, my agent, whom I love very much and who, somehow, is the biggest fan of every manuscript or sliver of idea I send her way. Thank you for being so steadfast. To Rebecca Mix for every writing date, even if we spend half of it talking. This author thing is hard, but it's a lot easier with you.

To Reina Galhea, Nidhi Pugalia, and Norma Rahal for one perfect first annual writing retreat weekend that I spent reshaping this entire book. First week of May, see you all there. To Mohammad Qasem for answering every medical question I had, even the hypothetical ones that had no answers. Especially those. To Norma Rahal, Kate Vinkovich, my siblings, my parents: family who never run out of encouragement or kind words or love. I love you always.

To Nidhi Pugalia. I'm proud of this book and that's because of you. Thank you for listening to every voice note, for reading every scene, for every thoughtful edit and insightful question. For being there when this book was barely an idea and talking me through it. You understood the shape of this story as I was still forming it and somehow helped me get that on the page. I love you and that'll never pass.

In the summer of 2016, Omar Radwan and I found a painting of an idyllic landscape in an ornate gold frame on a sidewalk in Brooklyn. The edges were chipped and damaged, the canvas fragile and old. It was at least as tall as me, and both of us knew we had to take it home. We painted the canvas white and used it as the screen to Abi Inman's (♡) projector. We've since bought a TV, but we've taken this painting to every apartment and house we've lived in since. Eventually, the idea, this book, would come. So, to Omar Radwan, who found this with me, and believed in what it could be. Who somehow always does.

About the Author

Meriam Metoui is the author of *A Guide to the Dark,* which *School Library Journal* described in its starred review as "Compelling . . . readers will have trouble putting this one down even for a minute." Born in Tunisia, she now lives in Detroit, Michigan, with her partner and her puppy. She is a graduate of the University of Michigan and Hunter College, where she received a master's degree in English literature. When not writing, she can be found behind a camera, obsessing over a new TV show, or wondering what hidden pockets of magic to write about next.

MeriamMetoui.com
@MeriamMetoui

CREDITS